DETECTIVI

GERALD HAMMOND SAUCE FOR THE PIGEON

by the same author

THE REWARD GAME
THE REVENGE GAME
FAIR GAME
THE GAME
COUSIN ONCE REMOVED

GERALD HAMMOND
SAUCE FOR THE PIGEON

St. Martin's Press
New York

Library of Congress Cataloging in Publication Data

Hammond, Gerald.
    Sauce for the pigeon.

    I. Title.
PR6058.A55456S2   1985   823'.914   85-2669
ISBN 0-312-69977-8

First published in Great Britain by Macmillan London Ltd.

First U.S. Edition

10 9 8 7 6 5 4 3 2 1

ONE

Keith Calder came whistling down the farm road and turned in through the gates of Briesland House. On the face of it he did not seem to have much to be whistling about. He had been up well before dawn on a freezing winter's morning, and instead of spending the day among his beloved guns, ancient and modern but preferably the former, he was due to spend it at the shop, stock-taking. Keith, who had once been itinerant in body and spirit, had come to terms with life as a settled businessman, but the humdrum chores of business bored him out of his mind. Those, in his opinion, were what partners were for.

However, the woodpigeon were here in great flocks, and to the dedicated shooter that fact was enough to mark the day in the reddest of letters even if most of it were to be spent in the dentist's chair – another engagement for which Keith had little enthusiasm. A couple of hours' shooting over decoys at the market garden had been rewarding. The bag of decoys on his left hip was balanced by a heavier bag of real pigeon on his right.

Keith was not a religious man but he had been known to thank his maker for the evolution of that perfect quarry, the pigeon. Requiring no assistance from man to proliferate in the wild, an enemy to the farmer who could be counted on to welcome its pursuer, a cunning and observant quarry demanding skill in fieldcraft and a high standard of shooting to bring to bag, the woodpigeon is the standby of the majority of shooting men.

And Molly was a great hand with the tough and earthy little bird. Her pigeon pilaf was a particular delight; but jugged or curried, jellied or in cranberry sauce, and especially in a pie with mushrooms and cider and flavoured with bay leaves, the pigeon was enjoyed by the Calders. Keith began to salivate at the thought.

Brutus, the black labrador, caught Keith's mood and frisked at heel.

They entered the house from the rear. Keith's mood might have spoiled if he had seen the car which waited at the front door. Instead, it rose higher. Molly, from the kitchen window, must have seen him coming. He could smell bacon frying. There would be eggs and coffee and toast and marmalade. With such a breakfast to round out such sport, he might even be able to face a day with Wallace without snarling more than once or twice.

The warmth of the house was stifling after the freezing air outside. Keith dropped his steamed-up sunglasses, his scarf, gloves and balaclava on the hall table. He leaned his bagged gun in a corner over his bags of birds and decoys. On to the hall chair went his cartridge belt and layer upon layer of warm clothing; for decoying is static, chilly work. Slippered, comfortable and half his former bulk, he went through to the kitchen.

Molly was putting his breakfast on the table. His daughter, Deborah, was in her chair. Brutus had already settled happily in the warmest corner, safe out of the way of feet.

And Chief Inspector Munro was dawdling over a cup of coffee.

Keith's euphoric mood began to waver at the edges. He ran a quick mental check over his various permits and licences. Everything from the car's MOT to the dog licence was up to date. True, he lacked a Game Licence, in company with almost everybody of his acquaintance, but after all, he had not been shooting game. Stolen goods turning up at the shop, then.

'Come to take me away, have you?' he asked.

Chief Inspector Munro did not smile. He was a lean Hebridean with a Calvinistic view of life and a supreme contempt for the habits and morals of all Lowlanders. Over the years, he and Keith had bickered into a relationship which somehow managed to blend antipathy with mutual respect, verging occasionally on qualified affection.

'I have come to ask for your help,' Munro said in his careful West Highland lilt. 'Real help, not "helping us with our enquiries".'

'A stolen gun?' Keith asked. He dropped into his chair and filled his mouth.

Munro shook his head impatiently, enhancing his slight resemblance to a peevish horse. 'A dead man,' he said. 'Found in a burning Land Rover, and a bag of pigeons nearby.'

That made sense. Reluctant as the police were to consult lay experts, there were certain matters of ballistics as applied to shooting in the field on which his opinion was sought from time to time. He was becoming experienced in the arts of the expert witness.

This could be anywhere in southern Scotland. He emptied his mouth. 'How long will I be away?'

'Not long. This one is just a few miles up the road. The body is too burnt to identify, without we know which dentist to ask. I was hoping that you might be able to put a name to him from other evidence.'

'The Land Rover's registration no good to you?' Keith asked between delicious mouthfuls.

'There is a fault on the line to Swansea. All this snow, doubtless.'

'Likely. Shall I take my car or will you bring me back?'

'I'll bring you back.'

'Hang on a minute, then.' Keith finished his bacon and eggs. While he buttered his toast, he spoke to Molly. 'Would

7

you call the shop? Tell Wal to carry on without me.'

Molly's attractive and usually amiable face managed to work up quite a creditable frown. 'But you'll be back soon?' she protested.

'Tell him you don't know when I'll be back.'

'Well, I think that's despicable. Just because you don't like stock-taking. He can't do it on his own and watch the shop, and you won't let him close up during the season.'

'Tell him to call in Minnie Pilrig to help out. Oh, and Molly, there's a few pigeon in the hall. They'll go off if they're left in the bag. Will you deal with them?'

'I suppose so,' Molly said with a sigh.

Keith reached over and ruffled his daughter's hair. 'A pity you can't help yet, Half-pint,' he said.

When the two men were gone, Molly fetched Keith's bag from the hall and laid out the pigeon on the kitchen table. 'Let this be a lesson to you about men,' she told Deborah. 'When your dad says a few, it all depends what he's talking about. If it's pounds on the housekeeping, it means two or three. But if it's drinks, or birds for me to pluck, few means anything from twenty up.'

Plucking would take all morning and result in a kitchen full of feathers. Freezing them in the feather only postponed the evil day and there was already a bag of feathered pigeon in the freezer. Instead, Molly set to and sliced out the breast meat. The now shrunken carcasses she dropped whole into a bin-bag and deposited it in the freezer until the day the dustbin-men called. By the time they started to thaw, they would be somebody else's problem.

A uniformed sergeant was at the wheel of Munro's police Jaguar. Keith and the chief inspector shared the back seat. The car turned north, away from the town of Newton Lauder, and soon took to a small road which continued northwards, climbing along the bottom of the valley and running roughly parallel to the main Edinburgh road higher up. Their road

8

went nowhere, Keith knew, except to serve a straggle of farms up to the valley's head among the moorland.

'From what I hear,' Munro said, 'you shooting men are all after the pigeon just now. I thought we were at the height of your season for the pheasant and grouse and so on.'

'Grouse are just about over,' Keith said patiently. 'With this hard weather there's a statutory ban on wildfowling, and the shoots are more concerned about keeping their birds alive than killing them. But we've had two mild winters for the pigeon population to build up, and now that the high ground's under deep snow, which we've more or less escaped, the pigeon are down here in hordes.'

'Is that so?' Munro said doubtfully. 'I have not seen them myself.'

'For God's sake, look at them,' Keith said. He pointed out a flock of more than a thousand pigeon, all heading south above the trees which lined the left side of the road.

'I see them now,' Munro said. It was almost an apology.

Higher up the valley, the car pulled in to the roadside behind two small panda cars and an ambulance. They got out. Keith was glad that he had resumed most of his warm clothing. Munro seemed to be impervious to the cold.

'I'll tell you this for a start,' Keith said. 'You needn't hope to get the dead man's name from the farmer. This is Andrew Dumphy's land. His kale's being hit hard by the pigeon. When the snow comes, it often happens that only the cattle-crops are left showing. The pigeon can clean them right off, leaving the farmer to buy feed for the rest of the winter. Mr Dumphy put the word around that anyone was welcome to shoot pigeon on his ground for as long as the snow lasted.'

'He told us just that on the phone,' Munro said.

They walked up a rough track, slithering where the light snow had penetrated the canopy of trees. The track took a twist between two sudden outcrops of rock.

'Just ahead,' said Munro.

'I can smell it.' Keith paused and sniffed, then walked on. They rounded a bend and came in sight of the still smouldering wreck. Keith had expected to see damage, but he was shocked to see that the Land Rover was almost wrenched apart. It stood on a circle of incinerated ground, the pine needles still smoking. Two ambulance men and a uniformed sergeant were standing by, but Keith could see other figures between the trees, scouring the ground.

'Forensic work can't begin until this mess cools down,' Munro said, 'but if you come this way . . .'

'Hang on a moment,' Keith said. 'Let me get the picture first.' He walked slowly around the Land Rover, using his eyes a little and his nose a lot. The smell of petrol was in the air, but he would have known it for a petrol model without that – the carburettor showed under the gaping bonnet. There were other smells. Burnt rubber and plastic and paint. Hot metal. Scorched bushes and the branches overhead – some of the trees, he thought, would have to be lopped or die-back would kill them.

Threaded among the other smells was one that was more awful because of its acceptable familiarity – the smell of burnt meat. The body crumpled across the front seats was far from recognizable. It was no longer a person but a thing, inanimate but shocking.

There were still more scents, but around the Land Rover they were drowned. Keith did a tour of the surrounding bushes. The heat had brought out the smell of the evergreens, but on a dead limb he thought that he could make out faint traces which were familiar.

'All right,' he said. 'What else have you got?'

'This way.' Munro led the way, Keith and the sergeant following, to where an empty bag lay beside a group of boulders. The bag's contents had been laid out on a sheet.

'Your groundsheet?' Keith asked.

'Yes.'

10

'May I handle these things?'

'Not the cartridges,' Munro said. 'They have still to be tested for prints. As to the rest, go ahead.'

Keith squatted down. 'Twenty-two woodpigeon,' he said, weighing one of them in his hand. 'They seem to be in good condition despite the weather. Two collared doves. One feral racer, at least I suppose it was feral, there's no ring on its leg. Eleven of the rubber-tipped sticks that decoys sit on, so wherever his decoys are or were the ground's too hard to push in a stick. Which, just now, is about everywhere. And twenty-eight cartridges, all of them fired. Twenty-five birds for twenty-eight cartridges is damn good shooting, unless he was shooting his birds on the ground. And always assuming that he gathered up all his spent cases.'

'Those cartridges,' said the sergeant. 'They aren't all the same.'

'This is Sergeant Bannerman,' Munro said, without suggesting that the information was of more than passing importance. In Munro's private version of the Police Manual, sergeants were to be seen and not heard.

'Hullo,' Keith said. 'That's very quick of you, Sergeant. You're right. The firing-pin marks are different.'

The sergeant debated with himself whether to take the credit for such advanced observation but decided in favour of frankness. 'It was the cartridges themselves I was looking at. They aren't the same make.'

'Ah. Don't pay attention to the printing. Shops often get their own names printed on the cartridges they sell. The bases are all Eley, and they're all twelve-bore, two-and-three-quarter-inch. There wouldn't have been a ha'p'orth of difference between them.'

'Except for the imprints of the firing-pins?' Munro said.

'Don't rush me,' Keith said. He went down on his knees and with a pen from his pocket he pushed the empty cases around. He bent right down to sniff at each cartridge. 'Of

11

course,' he said at last, 'some of these could be left over from a previous trip. Otherwise I'd say that we're looking for two men. These—' with his pen he isolated twelve cartridges '— have all been reloaded, you can see from the shape of the base. Five different printings. They've been fired from a gun with a flat instead of a round firing-pin, so that the imprint is a slot instead of a round hole. What's more, although the smells are very faint – because of the cold, I suppose – they smell of black powder rather than of modern smokeless. Which suggests to me that we have a man with a beloved old hammer-gun which has never been proved for anything stronger than gunpowder, so he loads his own cartridges with that, rather than risk damage to the gun or himself.'

'And the others?'

'The others are all Eley Grand Prix factory loads, number six shot. They've been fired in a modern gun. Not a repeater, you can see the ejector marks.'

'Two men, then?'

Keith shrugged. 'You'll need to look at them under a microscope to be sure that there's only two guns involved. And, remember, people do collect each other's empties to pass on to a friend who loads his own. We may have two men here or we may not. Was any gun found?'

'Not so far.'

'I see.' Keith got to his feet and straightened his back. 'I suggest that your forensic boys recover the shot from those birds and see how many makes and sizes there are. Have you found his decoying position?'

The two policemen looked blank.

'We'd better start from the beginning.' Keith took a seat on a rock which was slightly warmed from the fire. Munro hesitated and then chose himself a seat. The sergeant stood. 'The pigeon's a canny beggar,' Keith said. 'You can't drive it or walk it up like a game-bird. You've got to be as crafty as the bird itself to get near it. Sometimes you can wait on their

12

favourite flight-line, or in their roosting wood of an evening. But the only way you'd get a bag this size at this time of day would be by shooting over decoys from a hide. The pigeon's a gregarious bird, and if it sees what it thinks is a flock on the ground it's likely to join it.'

The sergeant sniffed. 'Doesn't sound very sporting,' he said.

'It's sporting all right,' Keith said. 'It needs fieldcraft, and it takes a good shot to shoot pigeon in the air.'

Munro waved aside these irrelevancies. 'There are no decoys here,' he said. 'Would they have burned up in the fire?'

'They might, if he had two bags and he put the other one into the Land Rover first. But this was his decoy bag. If he had two bags, one of them would be the standard game-bag of heavy canvas, and he'd have put his birds in that.

'On the other hand, he might do what I sometimes do; take a bag with his decoys and gear, a beltful of twenty-five cartridges plus a few in his pocket, and his gun. That's quite enough weight to carry until you know whether you're going to get lucky.

'He seems to have found a good spot. When he had some birds and was getting short of cartridges, he'd have to decide whether he was knocking off or going on. Either way, he'd go back to his vehicle.

'On the whole, I'd guess that he was ready to quit, because if you're going on you usually leave your shot birds out to add to the pattern of decoys. You may find that his decoys are still out in the fields somewhere, perhaps even complete with more birds and more empty cases. In which event, I'd say that he was going to go on and only came back to the Land Rover for more cartridges, and brought his surplus birds to save another trip later.'

'There are no signs of footprints in the snow,' Munro said. He seemed to be thinking aloud. 'Under these trees there is

13

no snow to speak of, just pine-needles, which take no prints. I suppose it will do no harm to have the men tramping about and searching. Just what would they be looking for, though?'

Keith got to his feet. 'Let me have a peer around,' he said. 'I may be able to save you some time.' He set off towards the splash of grey-white sky which marked the gap in the trees where the track reached the fields.

The other two followed behind. Munro spoke softly to his sergeant. 'If he gets his teeth into this thing, we may have to hold him back.'

The sergeant nodded. 'Let him help while we need him, sir,' he said. 'I can just see some of our stupid beggars tracking each other through the snow for the rest of the week. We could use a short cut.'

'Just as long as we know what's being cut,' Munro said.

From the edge of the fields Keith looked around, but the contours left large areas of dead ground out of his view. He climbed on to a fallen tree and looked over the fields, concentrating on the area to his left, back down the valley. The two policemen waited patiently, their heads level with his knees.

'I was shooting rabbits up here during the summer,' Keith said, 'so I know the ground. Since the hard weather came in I've been fully occupied with the market garden. My permission there requires that I shoot it twice a day if asked, and by God I've been asked!' He switched his attention to his right. 'Very odd!' he said. 'Pigeon flight to and fro between their feeding ground and their roost. These trees here are the favourite roost, as you'll have seen.'

'Will we?' Munro said.

'Look at the droppings, for God's sake! Now, as I remember it, Andrew Dumphy had his kale planted down there.' Without looking round, Keith pointed to his left. 'I'd expect anybody decoying to be over there or somewhere along that line, but I can't see any sign of decoys and the

14

pigeon aren't showing any interest in anything on the ground. On the other hand, away up the valley I don't see any pigeon flying at all, but I can see one sitting very still in a tree and there's a crow down in the field. I think we should go up that way. Feel like a walk?'

'How far is it?'

'About a mile. But there's a farm road if you want to take the car up.'

'We'll take the car,' Munro said.

The Land Rover was still smoking as they passed it.

In Munro's car, the sergeant spoke over his shoulder. 'Why would the man park there and walk all this way?' he asked doubtfully.

'Several reasons,' Keith said, 'depending on the man's thinking. He might have parked to take a look around, and then walked rather than scutter with moving the Land Rover. Or maybe he doesn't want to meet the farmer, doesn't get on with him . . . Turn left here . . . More likely he didn't want to block off the farm road, in case the farmer wanted to get a tractor out.'

The car bumped on to the farm road. The line of trees turned with them, but the overgrown conifers gave way to a mixed woodland of deciduous trees and pines.

'Stop here,' Keith said when they were a hundred yards up the side-road.

Munro was leaning over to peer out of the car. 'There's a pigeon up there in that tree,' he said.

'That's the one I was looking at from where we were,' Keith explained patiently. 'It still hasn't moved. I think it's a decoy, a "lofter", put in the tree to complete the realistic pattern. That's what the catapult in the bag was for. You fire a weight over a branch, to take over the end of a fishing-line, and pull it up. I wonder why he chose that pine when the deciduous trees are bare.'

'The fact remains that he did so,' Munro pointed out.

Keith nodded. 'Perhaps he knew it for their favourite sitting tree. There's no explaining the fancies of pigeons. You see those grey dots out in the field? Those are his decoys. And that crow further off, on the crest of the rise, that's a decoy too. A flock of pigeon looks more natural and more reassuring with a crow nearby. Let's take a closer look.' Keith made to get out of the car.

'Sit where you are, Mr Calder,' Munro said sharply. 'I can't have you trampling over everything before we have searched in a proper manner. I brought you out here to suggest names to me, no more than that.'

Keith sighed in exasperation. Munro often had that effect on him. 'You're tying my hands,' he complained. 'If I could look for the tracks of a dog, or see what make of decoys he was using or what kind of string or fishing-line or how he hid himself, I might be further forward. Are you treating this as a murder?'

Munro hesitated. 'It is an unexplained death,' he said.

Keith knew the signs. 'But are you treating it as a murder?'

'Until we know otherwise, yes.'

'And you're handling it yourself?'

'For the moment.' Munro tried not to scowl and succeeded instead in looking fretful. 'There would have been a chief inspector from Edinburgh here by now, but that Soutra is still blocked with the snow. We seem to have got off lightly, down here. Now, that is enough of the blethering. What names can you suggest to me?'

'Without taking a look around here, I can't get very far,' Keith said. 'Just look at what we've got. A petrol Land Rover, which may have been borrowed. There was an ex-Government sale not long ago, and a number of petrol models were sold around here. A thousand saved on the price of a diesel vehicle buys a lot of petrol. He may have been alone or there may have been two of him. He may have

16

been a good shot or you may find a hundred empty cartridges lying around. There may have been a dog, but maybe not. I could make a guess at most or all of those things if you let me look around.'

'Later.'

'All right. But if you even bring me one of his decoys, I might be able to tell something by its age and make.'

'Not yet.'

Keith sighed in exasperation. 'At least mind and photograph everything where it is,' he said. 'There could be a lot to be learned from the positions of things.'

'That much I can do,' Munro said. 'Now tell me about those cartridge cases.' When Keith hesitated, Munro went on with a sharpness underlying his soft, West Highland drawl. 'I know there is something already in your mind, Mr Calder. I know you of old. If you hold it back it will only look all the worse when it comes out, which in the end it will.'

'The only reason I'm shy of rushing in,' Keith said, 'is that I don't know a damn thing. Take the cartridges. They may have been left over from a previous trip. Or he may have begged some of them off somebody else so that he could reload them – although I doubt it.'

'Why?'

'I'll tell you, and then maybe you'll see how you're pushing me into the wildest guesswork. Around that Land Rover, even over all the reek, I thought I could distinguish two particular smells because they were familiar to me. They were black powder and modern smokeless powder, the two smells which I could make out in those cartridge cases. The smell round the Land Rover could have come from more cartridges, but it'd need one hell of a lot of them. And cartridges don't go off with much of a bang unless they're confined in the chamber of a gun. That Land Rover was just about shattered. Of course, you may find traces of some other explosive. But if not, if that damage was done by the

17

two types of shotgun propellant, there must have been a lot of it, and confined in tighter containers than plastic cartridges. So I'm guessing that there were tins of each in the back of the Land Rover. So there's a probability that somebody was going to do some reloading.'

Having set Keith talking, Munro was reluctant to interrupt. But he had an objection. 'Our man could have been carrying those powders for somebody else, could he not?'

'I wouldn't think so. No stockist would be happy to hand over gunpowder to somebody using Form F made out in somebody else's name. And you'd be twisting the long arm of coincidence, because some of those empty cartridges had already been reloaded at least once with black powder and fired in an old hammer-gun. You've a hell of a job to buy black-powder cartridges these days, so if you want them you load your own. And if you load your own you don't give away your empties.'

'Who—?' Munro began. In his impatience he drew the word out like a fog-horn. He began again, more softly. 'Who loads cartridges with gunpowder for an old hammer-gun?'

'Give us a chance,' Keith said. 'Lots of men around here have old guns which have never been proved for nitro. If you want to shoot with a really good gun and can't afford to pay thousands for it, you can get the same quality much cheaper in a gun which has only been proved for gunpowder. Of course, many of them just take a chance and use modern cartridges. But if you're conscientious you use the propellant which the gun was designed for.'

'When you get talking about guns,' Munro said, 'it is a hard job to stop you going on for ever. But if I want you to talk about people, you hardly say a word. I am asking you one last time. Who, around here, loads his own cartridges with gunpowder?'

'I do, for one,' Keith said. 'My partner and I share a pair

18

of vintage Lancasters, when we can get out together – which isn't very often, the business being what it is. Sir Peter Hay has a grand old Purdey, but I supply him with cartridges.'

'Who else?'

Keith hesitated. But the thought which had been cowering at the back of his mind would have to be brought out some time. 'Jake Paterson . . . for one,' he said.

'Paterson? The man who has the radio and TV shop? I don't remember him having a shotgun certificate.'

'He had one three or four years ago, because I sold him his gun. Knowing Jake, he won't have let it lapse. He's a pigeon-only man, plus occasional clays just as a relaxation. He's a bit of a loner by nature.'

'Sergeant,' Munro said, 'go for a walk. Don't disturb anything.'

Keith experienced a fresh prickle of interest. Munro was a strict officer who acted by the book and expected his subordinates to do the same. But, once in the bluest of blue moons, when his stern conscience told him that the book was in conflict with justice, Munro would throw the book over his shoulder and do what he thought was right, although never openly flying in the face of the law which he served.

'The remains in the Land Rover were too small to have been Jake,' Keith said when the driver's door had closed with a petulant slam.

'That is what I thought. But you can never be sure until you take measurements. A body loses a lot of bulk in a fire. Tell me what you know about Paterson.'

Fair enough, Keith thought. 'Jake's the cleverest devil I know,' he said. 'At thirty, he was the top designer for one of the country's top electronics manufacturers, and he dragged them out of the rut into a leading place in the world market. Jake ended up with a nervous breakdown. He'd been doing a three-ulcer job on a two-ulcer salary, and I think his ulcers were beginning to grow ulcers on their ulcers. So he chucked

19

it up.

'He thought he could settle down to life as a small-town shopkeeper, but he couldn't.'

'The world beat a path to his door?' Munro asked, with unusual poetry.

'He gets consulted a lot,' Keith agreed. 'But it isn't so much that. You just can't stop an active mind. Jake keeps getting ideas. He works them up and patents them, they get manufactured under licence and Jake makes another bomb. Christ, he could *buy* Newton Lauder if he wanted it. But his eyes are always on the next inspiration. From the signs, and from what I hear, he's putting together something earth-shaking just now.'

'Does he have a Land Rover?'

'Not that I know of. I've only seen him with a Lotus.'

'Does all this—' Munro nodded out of the car's window '—look as if he was responsible?'

'He shoots over decoys,' Keith said. 'And he uses a crow and a lofter, but so do most of us. His pattern of decoys usually looks more open than that one. But if you find that one of those decoys is a radio-operated flapper, then I'll maybe believe that that's Jake's remains in the Land Rover.'

'It takes two at least to make a murder just as it does to tango,' Munro said with grim humour. He seemed to search around in his mind. The Gaelic language is not rich in rude words, but he found one which would do. 'This is as awkward as the devil,' he went on. 'The man they are sending from Crime in Edinburgh is a Chief Inspector Russell. Does that mean anything to you?'

'Should it?'

'Perhaps not. No doubt you have seen our men walking about, or even driving, while tapping away at a thing which resembles a large pocket calculator. It is a device which was designed by Mr Paterson about two years ago. The patrolling constable need only press in the registration numbers of cars which he sees as he goes by. The device plugs into his radio, and another device in the station checks each number with the computer at Swansea. As soon as a number is found to belong to a stolen car, an untaxed vehicle or one regarding which an enquiry is out, the instrument buzzes and the vehicle's number shows up on the little screen.'

Keith made a mental note to check on the state of his car's tax disc. 'Very ingenious,' he said. 'But if some idiot's ever undiscriminating enough to nick my car—'

'No doubt,' Munro said without listening. 'Personally, I thought the thing excellent. But the point is that Mr Paterson offered his design to his former employers, who approached the Scottish Office who in turn consulted the Lothian and Borders police. The other forces, of course, were interested, but they left the testing to us. The job was given to Russell – he was with Traffic at that time – and he damned it as a useless and expensive piece of gimmickry. As far as the British police were concerned, it was dead. His old employers gave it up as a bad job. But Paterson persisted. He took it to the Japanese. Several overseas police forces became interested. One of them adopted it and praised it to the skies. Now it is on trial in two American states, Canada, Sweden and I-don't-know-where. So now all the British forces have production models to test. But if it is now adopted in Britain we will have to buy it back from abroad.'

'Which would make Chief Inspector Russell about as popular as a bleeding pile?'

'Less,' Munro said. 'Much less. The Scottish Office is only one of the bodies to call for his head, preferably with Russell no longer attached to it. As a consequence, he missed what was surely his last chance of promotion, and was moved sideways instead.'

'He won't like Jake very much,' Keith said.

'That is like saying that Hitler had a mild dislike of the

21

Jews. Russell has never been allowed to forget his error, by his superiors or by his colleagues. And I was hearing that his former subordinates in Traffic are very assiduous with their devices when they can be sure that he will see them.'

Keith was nodding. 'What you're saying is that the chief inspector who's on his way here is the one man who soothes himself to sleep with dreams of catching Jake Paterson in some illegal and preferably unnatural act and dragging him through the courts. Well, if the body is Jake's it may not matter. If it's not, then some other officer should be in charge.'

'It is very difficult to suggest bias until it has been shown,' Munro said, 'by which time it may be too late. Of course, the death may prove to be an accident. Vehicles have been known to catch fire at the moment of starting. And sometimes a man will start his engine first thing, so that the vehicle will be warm when he is ready to drive off. He may have intended to load up his stuff and then to drive nearer to where he was shooting before picking up his other gear.'

'It may be an accident,' Keith said doubtfully. 'But what if Russell refuses to recognize it as such? And what about the missing gun? That's the one thing a man wouldn't leave in his hide.'

Munro decided to tackle the easier question first. 'He could have put his gun down with the bag of pigeons, from where it was stolen by some vagrant who was drawn to the burning vehicle,' he suggested without any great conviction.

Keith had noticed the sergeant at the bonnet of the car. He was listening to his radio while scribbling clumsily in his notebook. Something told Keith that time was running out. 'You're suggesting that I see that Jake isn't railroaded,' he said, 'but you won't let me get a fair look at the evidence.'

'I never said—'

The sergeant was tapping on the window beside Munro. The chief inspector opened the door and shivered for a moment at the inrush of fresh air.

'Sorry to break in on you, Mr Munro, sir,' the sergeant said, 'but I thought you'd want to know this. The searchers have found a place where murder might have been done. Traces of blood on and around a fence. About mid-way between there and here, near as I can make out.'

Munro looked at Keith. 'Would that not be where a man is most vulnerable?' he asked.

'Could be. When you come to a fence, you most likely hand your gun to your companion. If you have one. And if you trust him. On the other hand . . . Was the fence barbed?'

'You're thinking that somebody may have gashed himself on the fence?' Munro suggested.

The sergeant permitted himself a smile. 'Hardly likely, sir. It was at a place where there was a split piece of plastic tubing slipped over the top strand of barbed wire.'

'Tubing?' Keith said. 'With a clip attached to one end?'

'They did say something about a clip, but I couldn't make it out.'

'Now I can point you towards an identity,' Keith said. 'There's one man around here who carries – or carried – a split tube which clipped on to his belt for ease of carrying. The tube let him swing his leg over a fence without tearing his clothes. I thought it a good idea. In fact, I'll copy it as soon as I get too stiff to vault a fence. It'd be safer for dogs, too – they can gut themselves on barbed wire. And if a dog decides to jump a fence while you're astride it you can lose a ball if your luck's out.'

'Come to the point,' Munro said. 'Who is the man?'

'If I ever knew his name, I've forgotten it. I've half-met him once in company, and then I met him again in the field and we chatted. He said he'd been a customer at the shop, although I didn't remember him. A small man, shorter than me and thin as a trout-rod.'

'Ah,' Munro said with satisfaction. 'That sounds more

23

like the corpse in the Land Rover.'

'I'm afraid it does. I think he lives in one of those ex-farmhouses further up the valley. You can track him down easily enough, because he holds a senior job with the concrete factory at Kalehead. I remember that he had a petrol Land Rover. I remarked that it wasn't exactly light on fuel but he said that it saved him a fortune in petrol because he could get to work the short way over the moors, while with a car he'd have had to go a hell of a long way round by road.'

'I am greatly obliged to you, Mr Calder,' Munro said formally. 'Sergeant Bannerman will take you home now.'

'Let me just have a look at the layout first.'

Munro got out of the car and then folded his lanky frame so that he could speak in through the door. 'I would not be able to explain a single unnecessary footprint to Mr Russell,' he said. 'Do not be worrying yourself. We will photograph everything and keep all that we can. Today we will be busy here and you will not be welcome, but the morn you can come back and nose about until your heart is content.'

TWO

Keith's car had vanished from the gravel in front of Briesland House, which suggested that Molly had appropriated it for a shopping trip. Keith stole a glance at the sergeant as the police car stopped. 'Would you lift me into Newton Lauder?' he asked.

The sergeant shook his head. 'I must get back for Chief Inspector Munro,' he said.

'Call him on the radio and ask him if he'd mind.'

'We're not running a taxi service, Mr Calder.'

Keith got out of the car. 'Tell Munro to give me plenty of time before he asks another favour of me,' he said. 'I want time to think up the rudest bloody answer anybody ever got. And I'm going to send him in a bill for my time as a consultant.'

'Do that,' the sergeant said. 'No doubt he will find a use for it.'

Keith slammed the door with all his strength, but nothing broke.

The sergeant, unperturbed, drove off. Keith let himself into the house, cancelled the burglar alarm and made for his study and the telephone, shedding outer garments as he went and fumbling for his pocket diary with its list of telephone numbers. He dialled the first number before he sat down. From Jake Paterson's shop he got an engaged tone. He rang Jake's flat and there was no answer after ten rings. He tried the shop again. Still engaged. Gabby bitch! Grinding his teeth in frustration, he dialled his own shop. His partner's wife answered.

'Janet? Keith. Where's Wal?'

'In the back, stock-taking. On his own.' Janet's voice was cold. 'Do you want to speak—?'

'No time,' Keith broke in. 'Something's badly agley and Molly's away with my car. Get Wal to come and collect me, now or sooner. You lock up for a few minutes and nip round to Jake's shop. That fat bag that works for him's got the phone tied up again. If Jake's there or in his workshop, get him out of sight. The police must not get their hands on him until we've spoken. Got it?'

'But—'

'Trust me,' Keith said, 'but trust me quickly.'

'Will do,' Janet said.

Without halting his fingers Keith managed to send up a brief prayer of blessing on Janet. Her quick mind and ready acceptance had saved his bacon before and no doubt would do so again. He tried both Jake's numbers once more, but there was no change. Too fretful to sit and wait, he put on his quilted waistcoat and his coat again, reset the alarms and walked down the drive. The day was still cold, but black clouds were coming up on a breeze from the south.

He met Wallace where the by-road which served his house joined what had once been a section of the main road but was now only a long loop-road through Newton Lauder. An extension of the old road ran on into the hills, passing the site of the burning Land Rover and petering out near where Keith believed the dead man to have lived. If the dead man were not Jake Paterson. Keith pushed the thought away and dropped into the passenger's seat.

'Thanks, Wal,' he said. 'Now, get me back to Newton Lauder as quick as you can.'

Using the mouth of the by-road, Wallace spun his small car and squirted away. Despite three missing fingers he was a good driver. The road ran almost straight and slightly downhill, and it had been gritted. Soon they were flat out. 'I hope all this haste is due to your eagerness to get back and

26

help me with the stock-taking,' Wallace said, 'but I'm not counting on it. Molly said something about a shooting accident. Anyone I know?' The absence of his usual stammer told Keith that his partner was annoyed.

'I'm not sure who it is, but, if it isn't Jake Paterson, Jake may be in dire trouble. I doubt it's an accident. Something smells bloody fishy, and there's a representative of the honoured fuzz who hates Jake's guts, stuck in a snow-drift on Soutra but heading in this direction when he gets through. We'll have a confabulation later. Drop me at Jake's shop for now.'

Wallace slowed the car as they approached the first houses and they threaded the streets of Newton Lauder at a comparatively sedate pace. 'Munro wouldn't let me take a good look round,' Keith said. 'And if those are rain-clouds ahead . . .'

'They'd be in line with the forecast. And I think it's warmer. A thaw's on the way.'

Keith said a rude word.

They passed through the square. The side on Keith's left was dominated by the Town Hall and the older part of the police building, but Keith leaned forward to see past Wallace. The sign in the shop door said 'Open'. Janet must be back, and business resumed. A hundred yards further on Wallace turned left, and soon stopped to drop Keith outside a double shop-front which bore up under the weight of three stone-built floors of flats above. As Wallace drove on to turn, Keith pushed into a shop crammed with space-age toys – televisions, music centres, computer games, CB radios, calculators of various degrees of sophistication, and, latest of status gimmicks, home computers which would not have disgraced a medium-sized business. A corner was devoted to the electronic security systems which were one of Jake's personal side-lines.

Predictably, the fat assistant was on the phone, exchanging scurrilous gossip with a friend while, with the aid of her spare hand, making inroads into a large box of chocolates. She had frizzed hair, a floral dress and spots, and her perfume cloyed the whole shop.

'Where's Mr Paterson?' Keith demanded.

The fat assistant scowled at him. Her face, he thought, could have modelled for the man on the moon. 'Do you mind, Mr Calder?' It was not a question but a rebuke from on high. 'I happen to be on the telephone.'

Keith leaned over and broke the connection. Her voice was shrill, but he shouted her down. 'You are tying up Jake's phone with personal calls while all hell's loose. If you want to save Jake and your job you'd better get your wits about you and tell me where your boss is.'

'I won't be spoken to—'

Keith found a few more decibels. 'You'll be spoken to a bloody sight worse if you don't get your finger out. There's a man dead and I've got to get hold of Jake in one hell of a hurry. Pull yourself together and tell me where he is.'

There was a moment's silence so absolute that it seemed to hiss. Then she said, 'He's away. On holiday. Abroad.'

'Since when?'

'Since this morning.'

Keith's instant of relief came to an abrupt end. 'You're sure that he got away? Tell me the details.'

'I don't see what . . .' She caught Keith's eye and deflated again. Keith was very angry and ripe for a major explosion, and it showed.

'Mr Paterson felt like a break in the sun. He made a last-minute booking, you get better terms that way. He leaves from Gatwick this evening. He told me yesterday that he was going to be up early, put in an hour at his shooting – sport, he calls it – and then drive south. He should be half-way to London by now. He's left me in charge for the next ten days. Satisfied?' Then curiosity overcame her indignation.

'What's going on?' she demanded.

'You'll know all about it too damn soon unless we're lucky. I must go now. When I'm gone, instead of calling your friend back, do your employer a service for once. Call Gatwick. Find out who he was to fly with. Leave messages for him, and make them as urgent as you can. He must, repeat *must*, phone me before catching his plane. I'll be at home from early afternoon until I hear from him.'

'I'll do that. Of course I will.'

Keith wondered whether to tell her not to reveal Jake's holiday plans to the police just yet. But, he decided, the police would soon find out about those plans and also about any attempt that he made to conceal them.

'You're sure that he got away?' he asked. 'He couldn't still be in his workshop?'

'He left the key with me.'

Outside the shop Keith turned left, entered another door and climbed one flight to Jake's flat. He knocked and rang and listened. There was no sound, no smell of gas or smoke, nothing to be seen through the letterbox. The place seemed dead. He clattered down the dull, utilitarian stair and into the street.

His watch said that the morning was almost gone, but could not tell him where. The dark clouds were overhead and the temperature had risen ten degrees.

Keith walked back to the square, where he found his wife stowing parcels in the boot of his hatchback. Deborah ran to meet him and he picked her up with an effort; she was growing heavier by the day. He had intended to reprove Molly for leaving him stranded, but she looked so good, and so pleased to see him, that he bit back the words. Instead, he filed them away, to be produced on the next occasion when Molly should point out his own selfishness.

'That's that done,' Molly said. 'How about buying us

lunch while you tell us all about the mysterious doings?'

This fitted in well with Keith's vague intentions, except that he rather hoped not to have to pay for the meal. His beginnings had been humble and impoverished, and, although he had now achieved a state of affluence which a few years before he would never have dared to imagine, something deep within him still rebelled at the concept of paying out good money for what could have been cooked at home.

'You pop on over to the hotel,' he said. 'I'll be with you shortly. Get yourself a gin, give Snookums whatever she wants within reason, wait five minutes and then order me a pint of Guinness – it takes forever to draw.'

Janet was still standing guard behind the counter of the deserted shop while Wallace wrestled with lists on clip-boards. Each was anxious for the latest news, but Keith had a prior call on his time. He made a bee-line for the telephone and dialled the number of the firm's solicitor. After a brief tussle with Mr Enterkin's secretary, whose mission in life was to protect her employer from clients, Keith got him on the line.

'You act for Jake Paterson, don't you?' Keith asked.

Ralph Enterkin's voice came booming over the wire. 'Two answers, my dear boy,' he said. 'First, it's none of your business. And, secondly, you know damn well I do. You witnessed his signature in my office last year.'

'Right. Now that you've picked that nit, I think your client's either dead or in dead trouble, probably the latter. How about lunch at the hotel?'

Mr Enterkin, who had a special relationship with good food, was tempted. But he was also conscientious. 'Couldn't you come over here?'

'Easily. But your good lady might have something to contribute.'

30

'I take your point.' Mr Enterkin's better half, as he rightly referred to her, had been a widow and a barmaid. Far from inviting her to quit her vocation, he had been delighted when she had taken up a post with the hotel. She had proved both popular and useful. She absorbed the local bar gossip like a sponge and, like a sponge, only gave forth when pressed. 'I shall join you there shortly,' Mr Enterkin said.

Wallace and Janet had been conferring. 'We're coming with you,' Janet said. 'You owe us a meal, and I haven't been able to make lunch for Wal because of you skiving off and leaving us stuck here.'

'What you really mean,' Keith said, 'is that you're dribbling down your chin with curiosity. But come along anyway. You may be able to help.'

They shut up the shop – a few minutes early, but who was to care? – and made their way across the square. A gentle rain had started. The chill was gone out of the air.

Newton Lauder's principal hotel had been fitted out in the mid-nineteenth century, to a very high standard even for that opulent period, and a wise management had refused to countenance any changes beyond essential repairs and replacements. Except in the public bar where, it was felt, standards might be allowed some minor relaxation, man-made materials were taboo and electronic entertainment was not to be thought of. It was a place of plate-glass, dark mahogany and muted sounds, and, if the young sparks considered it old-fashioned, their older and better heeled relatives found it a haven of peace.

When Keith arrived, with Janet and Wallace in tow, Molly and Deborah were already installed in a favourite place, a nook off the main lounge just large enough for two small tables which could be pushed together to seat six people in comfort. Apart from its privacy, its main attractions were the hatches from the bar on one side and

31

from the kitchen on the other. Molly was at the bar hatch, chattering to Mrs Enterkin. Deborah, in the hotel's genuinely antique high-chair, was spilling orange juice.

'Is my Guinness up?' asked Keith, whose habit it was to put first things first.

'I haven't got around to ordering it yet,' Molly said.

'Let's get around to it now. Hullo, Penny,' Keith added.

Penny Enterkin leaned through the hatch and cast her eye over the company. 'One pint of Guinness, two gin-and-tonics and a Glenfiddich. Is that right?' she asked in her comfortable West Country voice.

'A *large* Glenfiddich,' Wallace said. 'I only d-drink to keep up my strength.'

'And a large dry sherry,' said Keith. 'Your lord and master will be with us soon. Have one yourself and put them on our lunch bill. And, if you can, join us later for a few minutes. We want to pick your brains.'

Penny smiled. 'I don't know about brains, dear. But I'll join you if I can.' She turned away to fetch the Guinness from the further bar.

'She'll join us,' Keith said. 'The hotel manager worships the very ground she shakes.'

'I hope,' Mr Enterkin's voice said behind him, 'that you are not seeking to imply that either of us is, er, overweight?'

Keith felt his face grow hot. Molly was trying not to giggle.

'Just pleasantly plump,' Keith said.

And indeed the Enterkins were well matched, each having that jovial plumpness which comes from a full appreciation of the better and more fattening things of life.

'I should hope so indeed.' Mr Enterkin squinted down at himself. 'Sometimes I wonder whether I might not be the better for taking off a pound or two. And then I think of the agony of doing so and the absolute certainty that I should put it on again immediately. My doctor reminds me of the strain of carrying an extra load when I walk, so I combat that argument by walking less far but gaining more exercise from the weight I carry. Shall we sit down? All this walking is wearying on the feet.' Mr Enterkin had come all of a hundred yards.

A waiter helped them to push tables together. He took their orders and departed.

Mr Enterkin sipped his sherry. 'I'm told,' he said, 'that the police are much concerned about some vehicle found burning to the north of the town with a dead person still inside. I trust that you are not about to reveal that this was my client, Jacob Paterson?'

'I'll give you a quick run-down,' Keith said. 'This is a council of war. Those two are along to scrounge a free meal, and I've asked your missis to join us because she knows all about everybody. What I know is that Munro whisked me out to the scene this morning, in the hope that I could identify the dead man. He was in a short wheelbase, petrol Land Rover which seemed to have been blown apart from inside and then subjected to intense fire from the ruptured petrol tank. It might have been possible to make out the registration numbers, but anyway there was a fault on the line to the DVL place in Swansea, and most of the indications which might have pointed to the owner had been blown apart or burnt. It had been quite a bang, and yet the windscreen had been blown about twenty yards into a bush. It was scratched but not broken. I thought that I could smell both gunpowder and nitrocellulose powder around the wreck, and to back this up there was a bag nearby which held some dead pigeon plus a mixture of spent cartridges, some of which had been loaded with black powder and had the mark of a firing-pin which, to me, pointed straight away to Jake Paterson. There was no gun to be seen.

'I didn't want to point the finger at Jake, especially after Munro let out that the copper heading out from Edinburgh to take over the case hates Jake's guts, so I shilly-shallied for a bit. But I could hardly avoid mentioning his name.'

There were stricken faces around the table. Jake Paterson was a good friend. Molly put it into words. 'You don't mean that it was Jake's body? Jake doesn't have a Land Rover.'

'He borrows one sometimes,' Wallace said.

'I just don't know,' Keith said. 'Unless it was a freak accident, there were two men involved. Despite something that Munro said, I'd guess that the body was too small to have been Jake's. The police found a place where they think some kind of an attack could have taken place. It's beside a barbed-wire fence, and the top strand was protected by a split plastic tube. And that's a trick which I associate with a man I've met once or twice out shooting. A small man with a tired look about him. Small enough to have been the corpse. He certainly runs a petrol Land Rover. I think he lives in one of the converted farmhouses up Laurelrigg way, and works for the concrete factory at Kalehead.'

Discussion was halted while the waiter served them a meat course. As soon as he was gone Mr Enterkin spoke up. 'His name was Muir, Neill Muir. I say "was" on the assumption that you might for once be proved an accurate guesser. He did work at Kalehead, as their chief man of finance. He was taking an early retirement. I think his time was up a couple of days ago. He doesn't seem to have collected his pension for very long, poor chap.' Mr Enterkin's pudgy eyes managed to turn a piercing look on Keith. 'And why, may I ask, are you getting in a tizzy about a corpse of whose identity you aren't even sure?'

'I'm looking to you to tell me whether to get in a tizzy or not,' Keith said. 'Jake seems to be heading for foreign parts at short notice. What with that, and Jake's cartridges found on the spot, and a policeman whose life's ambition is to incriminate Jake taking over the case, there might be good reason for a tizzy if there was any connection between Jake and this chap Muir. So, do we panic or don't we?'

34

Mr Enterkin nodded slowly. 'If we are ever going to panic,' he said, 'now might be a very good time.'

Keith understood that it would not be proper for Mr Enterkin to say any more.

'I told that fat, female slob in Jake's shop,' Keith said, 'that she was to get a message to Gatwick for him, telling him to phone me before getting on his flight. And,' he added defiantly, 'I said that I'd wait at home this afternoon for his call.'

Wallace dropped his fork with a clatter. 'Why couldn't you have waited for the call at the shop?' he asked.

'Because I didn't think of it in time.'

Mr Enterkin protruded his lips in his habitual expression of deep thought and then nodded. 'I don't see anything more that can be done for the moment,' he said.

'No more do I,' Keith said. 'I was going to ask you to force Munro's hand to let me examine the ground. But the rain's on now, so it's too late.'

Molly looked up from monitoring Deborah's progress in transferring minced beef from her plate to various parts of herself. 'Too late for what?'

'Hang on a moment.' Keith bolted a mouthful of his cooling meal, swallowed and went on. 'I wanted to look at the ground, before the rain started to pee down, because there's something wrong. Not just a deader, although that's serious enough. The thing isn't what it appears to be. It's like one of those paintings of sailing ships which don't look right and you can't think why until you see that the wind's blowing the sails one way and the sea another and the pennants yet another way again. Whichever way I look at it, nothing adds up right. Take the decoy pattern. I didn't get the chance of a close look, which might have told me a hell of a lot more than it'll tell Munro or his pal from Edinburgh. At the time, there was a light sprinkling of snow over frozen ground. Now there'll just be mud.'

'The p-police will have taken photographs,' Wallace said.

'I hope so. But will they have taken the right ones? That pattern of decoys didn't look right for Jake or for Muir either. And if there's a copper on the way who hates Jake's guts . . .'

'Unless it was Jake in the Land Rover,' Molly said. Her brown eyes started to fill with tears.

'I think not. If he'd borrowed a Land Rover, his car would have been parked up the close beneath his flat; which it wasn't. So I think he left for his holiday.'

Mr Enterkin pushed his mouthful into one plump cheek. 'You always complain if I use Latin,' he said, 'but now you speak to me in Greek. What do you mean about a pattern of decoys?'

Keith raised his eyebrows. He seemed surprised that anyone in his close circle of acquaintances should be unfamiliar with the techniques of pigeon shooting. He glanced around the table. Wallace had finished his meat. 'You explain, Wal, while I catch up.'

'As told to children,' Mr Enterkin said. 'Remember that I am a child in these matters.'

Wallace pushed back a lock of lank, brown hair. His bony, intellectual face was solemn, for they were speaking of important rituals. 'The cushat – woodpigeon – is a wily beggar,' he said. 'M-maybe not quite as wily as a crow, but damn near. A slippery customer altogether. Also very difficult to shoot. They say that if you can shoot pigeon you can shoot anything.'

'If,' said Janet. As a farmer's daughter and Wallace's wife she knew about pigeon shooting and was herself more than a passable performer.

'The shotgun's essentially a short-range weapon,' Wallace went on. 'If you think of the limit as being forty yards, you won't be far out. So you've got to get within that s-sort of range. Their Achilles' heel is that they're gregarious birds. So the b-best and most favoured method is to find where

36

they're feeding or guess where they're most likely to feed, and put out a pattern of decoys which looks as like as possible to a feeding flock. Then there's a good chance that any passing birds will see them and drop in to join them.'

'You shoot them on the ground?' Mr Enterkin asked.

'That's not c-considered sporting. Now, your decoys will usually be plastic mouldings, shaped and coloured to resemble the real thing. Most people use half-shells, which are nice and compact to carry nested together.'

'Real birds are better,' said Janet. 'Fresh or stuffed or yesterday's birds out of the freezer.'

'True,' said her husband. 'But the plastic ones are usually on a stick with a rubber t-tip so that they bob in the wind like feeding pigeon.'

'Lending verisimilitude to an otherwise bald and unconvincing narrative?' Mr Enterkin suggested.

'Exactly. And most men have their own favourite t-touches to add that touch of verisimilitude. Like a decoy which flaps its wings when you pull a string, or a wire frame to hold a shot bird with the same end in view. And crows often hang around near a flock of pigeon, so a crow decoy nearby helps. And what's called a lofter – a pigeon decoy up in the branches of a tree, because there often is a bird up a tree, having a look round before dropping down, and other pigeon can see it for miles, sitting there and looking calm.'

'Very sneaky,' said Mr Enterkin.

'You have to be sneaky to get near pigeon,' Keith said. He pushed his empty plate aside. 'Thanks, Wal. The point is, we all have our favourite ways and tricks. Jake tends to scatter his decoys over a wide area, leaving a hole in the middle where he wants the live birds to come in and the shot ones to fall. This was a tighter pattern.'

'And Mr Muir?' Enterkin asked.

'I only met him the once that I remember. He used all those techniques. But what I remember most is the quality of his layout. I was short-cutting through a wood to where I knew there was some laid barley. Sure enough, when I came out of the trees there was a flock of pigeon only about thirty yards away. I expected them to go up with a roar, and I got ready. But they just stayed there, bobbing gently, and now and again one of them would give a couple of flaps. It took me . . . well, not a whole minute, but definitely some seconds to realize that it was a very well laid out pattern of decoys. The man was well hidden, too. This morning's pattern looked somehow stilted and mechanical, not the way that real pigeon congregate.'

'And the hide?' Molly asked.

'That's another odd thing. I don't remember a hide. In summer,' Keith explained to Mr Enterkin, 'you may get away with sitting down with your feet in a ditch and the weeds all round you, if your clothing's well camouflaged. But in winter, after the leaves are fallen and the frost's cut the weeds down, you'd be about as inconspicuous as the coalman's handprint on a white silk bum. No pigeon would come within a mile of you unless it was tired of life. So you build a hide with straw bales or camouflage netting, or whatever comes to hand naturally.

'And another thing,' Keith said, remembering. 'Neill Muir, when I met him, was using a flapper. It was a real bird in a wire cradle. Jake had a plastic flapper he bought from me. Jake being Jake, it was radio-operated by the time it was in use. But the point is, I let him have it cheap because it's not a design that would fool me if I were a pigeon. It was larger than life-size and the wings only went up and down, they didn't fold away. At best, it looked like a bloody great vulture coming across the field. I'd have noticed that all right. Jake said it worked quite well,' Keith added.

'Not Jake's decoys, then?'

'I'd say not. Doesn't help a lot, though, does it?'

Janet, for all her blonde prettiness, had a sharp mind

which was often one leap ahead. 'I've seen Mr Muir in the shop,' she said. 'He buys a lot of cartridges. Eley usually, although I think he took a box of Maionchi once when Eley had a strike or something. So I don't think he's a reloader.'

'Clever girl,' Keith said. 'No, come to think of it, when we introduced ourselves he said that he bought his ammunition from us.'

Mr Enterkin crumbled bread petulantly. 'I thought I was beginning to understand what you four were talking about – five, really, because that little bizzum is getting as bad as the rest of you—'

'She can name every gun in my rack,' Keith said proudly.

Mr Enterkin refused to be diverted. 'And now,' he said, 'you relapse into Greek again. Kindly expound.'

'What Keith's afraid of,' Janet explained patiently, 'is that this Edinburgh fuzz will jump to the obvious conclusion, or perhaps delusion would be the better word, that Jake and Mr Muir were shooting together, or maybe separately and they met at the fence, and that there was a quarrel, and that Jake killed Mr Muir and bunged him into the Land Rover and set it on fire in the hope of its being passed off as an accident. All that links Jake with it, apart from whatever it is that you're being so cagey about, is the presence of what seem to be his spent cases in Mr Muir's bag.'

Mr Enterkin was straining to keep up in this strange and sticky going. 'How do you know that it was Mr Muir's bag and not – God forbid! – Jacob Paterson's?'

'Jake carries a hessian sack for his decoys and birds.'

'And he's the only man around who shoots black powder cartridges?'

'He's the only one who uses them in a gun with that shape of firing-pin,' Keith said. 'As far as I know.'

'You'd know,' Molly said.

'It seems to be a lot of trouble to go to,' Mr Enterkin said, 'saving up empty cartridges, and buying gunpowder – which

I believe is harder to come by than the modern stuff – and loading up and so on. What's the point?'

Keith repeated, almost word for word, the explanation which he had given to Munro. 'That's why, just for the fun of it, Wal and I sometimes share a pair of old Lancasters. Wal shoots off the left shoulder, so I had to alter the cast of one of them for him.'

'Cast?' Mr Enterkin said. 'No, don't tell me. I can't absorb many more technicalities at the moment, and this one seems to be irrelevant. You were hoping that Mr Muir was also a reloader, using gunpowder?'

'I'm damn sure that he wasn't,' Keith said. 'I'd have known, as Molly said. We sell most of the black powder around these parts. But if Muir reloaded at all, even with modern powders, he might well have been saving up other people's spent cartridges. Has any one of you ever sold him powder or wads or shot or primers? Small, thin man, nearing fifty, with baggy eyes.'

'Straight, gingery hair,' Janet added, 'going grey at the sides and thin on top.'

Molly and Wallace shook their heads.

'I never saw him without his hat,' Keith said. 'Well, that's it, then. I can't think of a single innocent explanation for Jake's empties being in Muir's bag, except, just conceivably, that Muir was conscientious about tidiness – I noticed him picking up his own cases – and if he'd come across some of Jake's he might have tidied them up. But I doubt it, because Jake's a fanatical hoarder of empty cases, especially the yellow Maionchi ones, which he swears are the best for re-crimping. And there were several of those in the bag.'

Keith paused and looked hard at Mr Enterkin. 'That's all we know so far,' Keith said. 'And if there was no connection between Jake and Mr Muir you could tell me that I'm making a mountain out of a molehill and we could get on with enjoying our lunch. But you're not going to tell me that, are you?'

'No,' Mr Enterkin said sadly. 'I can't tell you that.'

The waiter served biscuits and cheese and coffee. Keith waited impatiently until they were private again. 'You may as well tell us what the connection is,' he said.

'And I may as well not,' the solicitor retorted. 'My client's affairs are private and may as well remain so. You have no need to know.'

Wallace James pointed a long finger at the solicitor. 'Perhaps you've n-no n-need to tell us,' he said. 'Jake has been raising money for some gadget of his own design, something in the radio line. I know b-because he asked me and I put him in touch with an investor. You t-tell us that Muir was a "man of finance". He was taking early retirement. Keith's guess is that he wasn't fifty yet. From what I hear on the accountants' grape-vine, the managing director of Kalehead wanted that job for some relative who's coming home from a post abroad. P-put that together and what does it smell of?'

'A bloody great golden handshake,' Keith said, 'and a man looking to invest in a new career.'

'And,' Janet put in, 'if he'd changed his mind, another man with a great big motive for losing his temper.'

Mr Enterkin was glowering. The expression sat badly on his cherubic and usually benign visage. 'I never made any such suggestions, and if you have any sense you'll forget that those words were ever spoken. Just accept that there is a connection, sufficient for me to share, to some extent, your unease. I trust that Mr Paterson's holiday was booked some time ago.'

'So did I,' Keith said. 'But no. Jake knows perfectly well that the price of a package holiday nose-dives during the last few days if there are unbooked places. If you go to a travel agent and say, "I can leave any day from now on, so send me somewhere sunny", you'll pay a fraction of the usual price.'

41

Mr Enterkin again protruded his lips in the thoughtful pout which, although familiar, was always startling. 'A pity,' he said at last. 'But even a booking made yesterday or the day before would suggest his innocence. Or premeditation, which in the circumstances would be unlikely.'

'What circumstances?'

'None of your business.' Mr Enterkin paused again for fresh thought. 'You, Keith, had best spend the afternoon hovering like a vulture over your phone. If and when Mr Paterson telephones, tell him that he must, without fail, speak to me before boarding that plane. If I'm satisfied that nobody is waiting for him, then it might be best if he were to proceed with his holiday. His total absence from sight, and from mind but for the arrival of the occasional vulgar postcard, might, for the next week or two, be the happiest solution. And, of course, his subsequent voluntary return would have just the opposite effect to the present symptoms of intended flight.'

He might have continued thinking aloud but for the arrival of his wife, carrying her own chicken-and-salad lunch. She took the chair beside her husband. Seen together they were an obvious match, two plump and jovial figures modelled by a maker in playful mood.

'Sorry I've been so long,' Penny Enterkin said, 'but the bars are busy, what with them all wanting to talk about Mr Muir being killed like that. Was that what you wanted to speak about?' Her Devonshire voice always sent little shivers of pleasure up her husband's spine.

'It is Mr Muir, then?' Keith asked.

'Seems so, my dear. At least, one of Mr Ledbetter's garage hands was called out to identify the Land Rover. He'd put on a new tow bar and replaced the windscreen last summer. He'd made the tow bar, so he could identify that. Terrible, he said it was. And the dentist was fetched away from his bar lunch a few minutes ago, so I dare say we'll know for sure before long.'

'Is the policeman from Edinburgh here yet?' Keith asked. 'I heard that he couldn't get through because Soutra was blocked again.'

'He'll be here by now, then,' Penny said. 'Soutra was cleared by eleven, because a rep from the brewers came in. He said that he followed the snow-plough as far as Carfraemill.'

They seemed to have said it all. There was a silence, broken by Molly. 'It's his widow I'm sorry for,' she said. 'Being dead can't be all that bad, but being left must be terrible. He did leave a widow?'

Penny had just filled her mouth. She nodded.

'If indeed it is Mr Muir,' said Mr Enterkin, 'he leaves a widow some years younger than himself. And larger. A positive Amazon. I believe that she was something of a sportswoman a few years back, representing Britain in some cup or other. Tennis or squash, or possibly badminton. You've probably seen a large, Nordic-looking blonde striding about the town.'

'I don't think she's often in the town,' Penny said. 'She gets her supplies in Edinburgh. But Mr Muir used to come in here from time to time, for a lager or a g. and t., and his wife came in with him once, earlier this year. A big, strapping blonde, my dear, just as you said.'

'I think I saw her once,' Janet said. 'In the chemist's. I can't believe there's two such Valkyries about the place. If I'm thinking about the right two people, they didn't look as if a man like him would be enough husband for a woman like her. Did they get on?'

Penny glanced at her husband before speaking. He raised his eyebrows. 'They seemed very lovey-dovey, the time they came in here,' she said. 'That's why I was so surprised when she came in alone about a fortnight ago, dressed up to the nines, or undressed down to them, whichever way you want to look at it, and look at it you certainly could. She was out for a pick-up, making eyes at all the men.' She looked at Keith. 'Went off with a friend of yours in the end. That Mr Paterson who has the telly shop. He's a widower, of course, and you could expect it of him, but . . .' She stopped dead, warned by some tremor in the atmosphere, and turned to her husband. 'Have I said something I shouldn't?'

Mr Enterkin patted her hand. 'Nothing that wouldn't have come out sooner or later,' he said. 'It's just as well that I know now rather than have it sprung on me. No point going over it all again, I'll explain when we have time. It looks, Keith, as though your fears were well founded. You had better go and man your telephone, and all that I said before now goes ten times over.'

Keith nodded. 'And if there's anything else that we can do to help . . .' His companions made acquiescent noises.

'Bless you!' Mr Enterkin said. 'Run along as soon as you're ready, and leave the bill to me. I'm deeply appreciative. Although just why you should want to help my rash and foolish client out of the mire which he seems to have created for himself I can't imagine.'

'We like him,' Janet said. 'He's a good person.'

'And a damn fine shot,' Keith added. That, in his book, would have excused anything from a lack of personal freshness to sodomy.

'And a good cash customer,' said Wallace. It was his accolade.

'I was friends with Nancy, his late wife,' Molly said gently. 'She was the nicest person I ever knew. When she knew that she was going to die, before she even told Jake, she asked me to see that he was all right. I haven't been able to do much, he doesn't need it. I've spring-cleaned his flat once or twice, because when he's absorbed in something new he lets it go, and I've nagged him to buy new clothes and made sure that he doesn't just eat out of tins. But I think Nancy rather hoped that I'd marry Jake.'

'Why didn't you?' Keith asked curiously.

'He never asked me.'

Keith thought that over. 'Oh,' he said at last.

.

THREE

Keith used his own key to make off with the car. Two, he thought, could play that game. Sauce for the goose. He drove, over wet roads but under a clearing sky, home to Briesland House. He took Brutus the labrador for a short, bladder-emptying walk and then tried to settle down. He was too early for the telephone message – even Jake in his Lotus could hardly be past London yet. But Keith wanted to be available at the earliest possible moment. There were certain matters which he wanted to raise with Jake before Jake spoke with Mr Enterkin. These included a tactful enquiry as to whether Jake happened to want an alibi . . .

Molly phoned. She was looking after the shop while Janet helped Wallace with the stock-taking. Keith gathered that his name was a dirty word around the shop. Wallace, Molly said, was muttering some quotation about twenty-nine distinct damnations and hadn't stammered once.

To soothe his impatience Keith settled to his favourite therapy. While Vivaldi from the four loudspeakers spread charm on part of his mind, he began the task of dismantling the latest addition to stock – a good but rusted fowling-piece by Rhoades with a lead ball firmly corroded into the breach. With a worm, patience, force and much bad language he managed the unloading. Then, with penetrating-oil and a hot screwdriver, he attacked screws which had not been loosened for a century.

But his attention was as restless as a butterfly. Whenever he looked up from his workbench it was caught and lured away, first by the rack after rack of antique guns with polished walnut and silver and plum-brown steel, and then

46

by the window. The first floor of Briesland House commanded a view down the valley to Newton Lauder and beyond. The frost was returning and the sky had cleared as if there had never been a cloud. A single crow hung in the void, one speck in the enormousness of space. Keith was reminded that the pigeon would soon be flighting to a favourite roosting wood. The lunchtime talk had reminded him of the sweet balance of the Lancaster hammer-gun, and he longed to take it, with a beltful of black powder cartridges, and to go and stand in wait for the fleeting shapes to jink above the treetops. It was at such times, or walking with dog and gun, that his mind worked freely.

His hopes died with the daylight. When the phone rang at last and Mr Enterkin's voice came on the line, the last strip of cold light was fading above the hills to the west.

'The worst has befallen,' Mr Enterkin said. 'The police removed Paterson from the departure lounge.'

'Under arrest?'

'Not yet, so far as I know, although it may only be a matter of time. I gather that he is isolated in a VIP lounge, awaiting the arrival of officers who are already on the shuttle from Edinburgh to Heathrow, and that much may depend upon what story if any he tells when they arrive. He does not seem to have asked for a solicitor.'

'I see,' Keith said. 'Any other news?'

'They have found what they believe to be Muir's gun, dismantled and thrown into the rhododendrons about a quarter-mile this side of where the Land Rover burned. I doubt if we shall hear more until the pathologists have finished with the – er – deceased.'

'How long is it since you heard the news about Jake?'

'About an hour.'

'You could have phoned me earlier.'

'I could,' Mr Enterkin said with asperity, 'except that I have spent virtually all of the intervening period on the

47

telephone to Gatwick, at first trying to speak to my client and then endeavouring to find out whether he had received my message and, if not, whether it had been aborted by the police so that they could intercept him in the act of boarding a plane bound for foreign parts. Not one of my efforts met with the least success.'

Next morning, Keith's agreement with the proprietor of the market garden required him to repeat his foray against the grey hordes. But the pigeon were shy and disbelieving and Keith's mind was not wholly on his task. He returned home, plucked his modest bag, ate breakfast and was heading into Newton Lauder by nine o'clock. He was happy to offer Wallace his help, now that he could be reasonably sure that stock-taking was finished.

It was far too early to contact Mr Enterkin, so Keith was astonished to learn that that notoriously late riser was already in his office and had been trying to reach him.

Keith crossed the square, climbed a flight of stairs and reached Mr Enterkin's office. The secretary was not yet on guard in the outer office, but he found the solicitor brooding in his inner sanctum, glowering at the tide of papers which always seemed about to engulf him. He looked up and took a second or two to focus.

'Sit down, my boy. Sit down.'

Keith took the only uncluttered chair. 'What news?' he asked.

'Little, and none of it good.' Mr Enterkin held up a chubby hand, preparatory to counting on his fingers. 'First of all, Paterson has been arrested and is being brought back today.'

'Oh dear,' Keith said mildly.

'You sum the matter up in a nutshell, although a long, low groan might have been more to the point. The police action seems a little precipitate unless something more than we already know has occurred to harden their suspicions. There could, of course, be a thousand things which will emerge later to confound us, but what jumped unwelcomed to my mind was that the first question to be asked of Paterson would have concerned his whereabouts shortly after yesterday's dawn. And I hope to God that he has not taken the dangerous step of proffering an alibi to the police before trying it out on his solicitor.'

'I'd have thought,' Keith said, 'that an alibi would be the best thing going.'

'The same thought may have occurred to Paterson,' Mr Enterkin snorted. He changed fingers. 'But alibis are notoriously difficult to prove and easy to break. And in the present case an alibi might well prove to be both a snare and a delusion. Consider for a moment. To whom would your friend and my client be likely to turn for an alibi at that unlikely hour?'

'Oh,' Keith said. 'A lady, you think?'

'A female person, at least. And just at the moment his name seems to be linked with that of only one person of the opposite gender. The dead man's wife. You see the predicament?'

'Clearly,' Keith said.

Mr Enterkin was not one to be stopped by the knowledge that his listener was ahead of him. He changed fingers again and rolled on. 'Either Paterson would do the gentlemanly thing and keep silent. Or he would place his liberty before both their honours and offer her name as his alibi, thereby immediately furnishing the police with a better motive, or one supplementary to the one already known to them. In turn, Mrs Muir would have to decide whether to support his alibi at the risk of suggesting to the police that they were in collusion, or denying it and thereby landing him even deeper in what I have heard you refer to as the clag, whatever clag may be.'

'Just mud.'

'I had hoped for something less savoury.' Mr Enterkin looked at his hands and lowered them. 'I've lost count,' he complained. 'Anyway, it occurred to me to telephone the proprietor of the fruit and vegetable shop near Mr Paterson's flat. His trade demands an unconscionably early start to the day. He informed me that yesterday morning, when he arrived to open his shop, he noticed in the close where Mr Paterson parks his car another vehicle, a hatchback of a particularly gaudy red – which description fits the only car in which I have ever seen Mrs Muir. She certainly refused, in my hearing, to set foot or any other portion of herself in her husband's Land Rover. He further told me that the police had already obtained that information from him.'

'She'll have to alibi him, then,' Keith said.

'My boy, you are still not thinking the matter through. In passing, some slight corroboration, if it is needed, is furnished by something overheard by my good lady in the bar last night. It was suggested that, prior to her marriage, Mrs Muir had a reputation which was far from virtuous. 'Man-mad' was the expression used.

'Finally, the police have sealed Mr Paterson's flat and also that part of his shop's back premises which he used as his personal workshop. It may be presumed that the thought has occurred to them, as it had to me, that Mr Paterson might have contrived to provide himself with an alibi while knowing full well that to cause an explosion and a fire some miles away would present no difficulty to one of his inventive talents in the field of radio.'

'That's not so good,' Keith said.

'Again, you understate. Knowingly or unknowingly, the lady provides herself with a perfect alibi without affording Mr Paterson any real protection whatever. Imagine it. The deed done the night before. The Land Rover bestowed in what I believe to be a secluded spot and the decoys distributed – all by starlight, which might well have caused those deviations from the norm which aroused your suspicions. A lady, who may be quite innocent, is welcomed to his flat and to his bed, already a widow had she but known it. Then, at a more credible hour, a hand under the bed or a trip ostensibly to the bathroom, the touch of a switch, and far away there occur an explosion and a fire which between them play havoc with the evidence.'

Keith thought it over, and the more he thought the less he liked Mr Enterkin's hypothesis. 'In that case, why would Jake's cartridges be in the bag?' he objected.

'Hopefully because that is not what happened. But it may well be the police theory, and we must prepare to refute it. The one tiny crumb of comfort is that Paterson has at last announced that he is saying not another word outwith my presence. Too late, no doubt, but it is all the comfort we have for the moment.'

'So what happens now?'

'Well, now.' Mr Enterkin laced his fingers over his round paunch. 'Much will depend on the autopsy findings. Assuming for the moment that there are any findings of significance – which, in view of the body's state, is far from certain – and that they are compatible with Mr Paterson's guilt, he will be brought here and taken before the sheriff, who will commit him for trial before the High Court in Edinburgh.'

'Must that happen?' Keith asked. 'Can't you put on a defence in the sheriff court?'

'You've been reading Perry Mason again,' Mr Enterkin said severely. 'The sheriff court proceedings are purely formal, being concerned with such matters as legal aid and representation, and then a pleading diet at which a date is set for the High Court. Arguments will only begin when he comes up for trial in Parliament House.'

Keith had had some experience of such matters. 'That

won't be tomorrow,' he said. 'Or even next month.'

'Dear me, no.'

'How long, then?'

'That depends on how long it takes to collect the necessary evidence, whether or not one side or the other is striving for delay, how many other cases precede his in the calendar and whether the accused in those cases decide to plead guilty. It can take a long time.'

'During which poor Jake languishes in the nick while he may be perfectly innocent. It doesn't seem very fair.'

'The law is not concerned with fairness.'

'Justice, then?'

'Only marginally with justice.'

'Then what is the law concerned with?'

'A good question.' Mr Enterkin repeated his moue of deep thought. He might have been sucking treacle through a straw. 'And, although I have been its servant for more years than I will admit to, I don't really know. To be frank, I think that the law is concerned only with itself.'

'Aren't we all?'

Keith would have pursued his questions further, because needling Mr Enterkin on the subject of the law's deficiencies was one of the pleasures in his life; but they were interrupted by sounds from the outer office and Mr Enterkin seized on his chance to escape. 'Miss Wilkes seems to have made a belated arrival,' he said. 'You'll take a cup of coffee?'

'I'd better be going. Is it all right if I go back and look over the ground?'

Mr Enterkin snapped his fingers. 'I knew that there had to be a reason for me to see you,' he said, 'other than answering all your questions. I just couldn't think what it was. Chief Inspector Munro advises me that the police expect to have completed their searches by mid-morning. If you think that there's anything to be gained, do by all means take a look. Despite your outrageous charges for such services in the past, I have to admit that you have always produced value for them at the end of the day. And I dare say that Mr Paterson can and should afford them.'

'I'll speak to Wal,' Keith said. 'If he doesn't mind holding the fort, I'll give all the help I can. Are the fuzz doing a search at the decoying site?'

'I think they've confined their intensive search to the area between the Land Rover and where they think that an attack may have occurred. At what you call the decoy site, I gather that only the most cursory search has been made. But they took copious photographs, at my insistence, before removing the decoys. They regard all that happened there to be irrelevant.'

'I'll get moving,' Keith said. 'It could snow again, and if that happens what few signs are left will be lost.'

'Would you mind if I came with you?'

'You?' Keith said with some surprise.

'Who else? You may well appear astonished, but duty calls. There would seem to be nothing useful that I can do here until my client arrives and is allowed to see me. On the other hand I shall be responsible, in due course, for taking precognitions and for briefing counsel, and it would be desirable, although in breach of precedent, if I were to have some idea as to what we're talking about.'

'Well, all right then,' Keith said doubtfully. 'I'll go over and square my absence with Wal. You go home and put on lots of warm clothing and some comfortable boots. I'll either be in the shop or at my car. You do appreciate that we may have to walk some distance in the course of searching?'

'I do,' Mr Enterkin said. 'I am resigned to it. But perhaps if you were to lend me a shooting stick I could take a seat while you make circles about me?'

'If you come,' Keith said, 'you help me search.'

'So be it,' Mr Enterkin said with a sigh.

FOUR

To Keith's surprise Wallace, although still plaintive, took a liberal view. 'For God's sake do all you can for Jake,' he said. 'A fee would be useful, but as far as I'm concerned it's not essential. The main thing is to get Jake off. If Molly helps out when she can, Janet and I can look after the shop. You just cope with the more urgent overhauls and the antiques side of things, and the rest of your time is Jake's.'

'Thanks,' Keith said. 'I hope you'd do as much for me.'

'I'd do as much for anybody who helped with the stock-taking,' Wallace said. From which, Keith gathered that he would be unwise to count on any such indulgence.

They filled a few minutes with business details.

Keith went out to his car when he saw Mr Enterkin arrive. The solicitor was wearing leather boots and a woollen hat. In between, his sheepskin coat had been dragged over layer upon layer of sweaters. He bulged even beyond his norm, to the point where Keith was doubtful about his ability to enter the car. The feat was achieved with much grunting and adjusting of seats, and was accompanied by a rapturous greeting from Brutus, who had once been Mr Enterkin's and remembered him as an indulgent owner. Keith always embarked the dog if there was prospect of much walking.

'That's the first time I've seen you in a sensible pair of boots,' Keith said as he drove off. 'I never thought I'd see the day.'

'Blame my wife. A farmer's widow before we married, you may recall. She much enjoys striding about the countryside.'

'And she drags you along with her?'

'She is not so cruel. The boots are hers. I have very small

54

feet, so we can exchange footgear on occasions. Not,' Mr Enterkin explained earnestly, 'that I am in the habit of donning her shoes, but she does usurp my slippers from time to time on colder evenings.'

'I warned you before you married that nothing would be sacred,' Keith said.

They drove north out of the town, climbing slightly up the valley bottom through farmland stark with the baldness of winter. Above them to their left, traffic crawled along the new trunk road which by-passed Newton Lauder. They had the former main road to themselves. They passed Briesland House and took to the minor road which continued north until it lost itself among the hills.

A panda car and a blue van stood, unattended, near where the Land Rover had burned. Keith drove on for a mile and parked at the mouth of the farm road.

They emerged into the cold air, the solicitor puffing and straining, and Brutus with a leap and a dance. 'We're not shooting,' Keith said. Brutus lowered his tail, but raised it tentatively when, after dressing as if for the shooting field, Keith slung a game-bag over his shoulder.

'For clues?' Mr Enterkin asked.

'You'll see.'

The woodland where the Land Rover had ended its useful life continued as a narrowing strip of trees along the roadside, and turned back alongside the farm road for a few hundred yards. Occasional hardwoods rose above the conifers. Keith regretted the loss of summer's foliage, but he had to admire the tracery of branches against the sharp blue of the sky. The farm road, which was narrow, had been tarred at some time in the distant past, but it was now a victim of weeds and potholes.

'If he was going to decoy here,' Mr Enterkin said, 'why didn't he park here?'

'Any number of reasons,' Keith said. 'So as not to block

the farmer in, which is why I parked out on the road.'

'Where is the farm?'

'Over the crest ahead. They won't have seen anything, but it might be interesting to ask whether they heard shots. What did you ask me?'

'Why he didn't park here.'

'Yes. He may have been on bad terms with this farmer and have decided to keep a low profile. Or he may have parked where he did, taken a look round, seen pigeon up this way and decided to hoof it rather than to bother starting up the Land Rover again. Also, there's no doubt that pigeon are warier around a parked vehicle.'

'You don't sound very convinced,' Mr Enterkin observed.

'I'm not. How many pigeon do you see around here?'

Mr Enterkin looked vaguely in the direction of a few birds in the field to their right.

Keith sighed. 'Crows,' he said. 'Black, with square wing-tips, slow beat, crows. Smaller, blue-grey, short, pointed wings with a quicker beat, pigeon. You needn't bother looking just now. They'll come back to roost in the trees down by that Land Rover this afternoon. For the moment, they're feeding. And there's bugger-all for a pigeon to feed on around here.'

'Those crows are feeding.'

'Probably worms. Crows eat almost anything. Pigeon are vegetarian. They'll be looking for kale or clover, likely.' As he spoke, something stirred in the remotest corner of Keith's mind. But they reached the end of the trees and the moment passed.

'This is about where Munro stopped the car,' he said. 'The decoys were out in the field there. Except for the lofter which was up in that Scots pine, for some reason unknown. It's meant to be as conspicuous as possible. That oak would have been better.'

Mr Enterkin looked up at a rowan. 'You spotted it from a

mile away,' he pointed out.

'True. But I was looking for it, and I saw it against the background of a snow-covered hillside. I wasn't looking from the same angle as a pigeon. There should have been a hide of sorts, but I couldn't see it. Let's take a look at the ditch.'

'Is there a gate?'

'Miles away.' Keith unslung his game-bag and hung the heavy canvas flap over the top strand of barbed wire. 'Be my guest.'

The shortness of Mr Enterkin's legs was no help, but, with the protection of the game-bag, he crossed the fence undamaged.

'You're a gentleman,' he said, puffing.

'It wasn't for your benefit but the dog's.' Keith flicked a finger and Brutus hurdled the fence. 'Sometimes they have to take their chance, but there's no point risking it if you don't have to. They can do themselves damage.'

'So could I.'

'That's why Mr Muir carried his split plastic pipe.'

The ditch was shallow and none too wide. They walked it for fifty yards in each direction. 'This is stupid,' Keith said. 'You could sit with your feet in the ditch all right, but at this time of year no pigeon would come within a mile of you. There's only one possible place within gunshot of those decoys.' He led the way to the last tree, a pine, which was split at ground level and sent up two slowly diverging trunks. 'You could wedge yourself in here and be inconspicuous,' he said. 'It wouldn't be good, but it'd do. But then, look here.' He bent and picked up two empty Remington shells. 'The police search was cursory all right.'

'Those are significant?'

'Only because Muir was a compulsive picker-up of empty cases. You could ask the police whether they found a camouflage net?'

57

'I'll do that.' Mr Enterkin pulled off his sheepskin gloves and dug deep into layers of clothing for a notebook. 'Might it not have burned in the Land Rover?'

'Possible but not likely. Well, we're not doing much good here. What with a black frost at the time, then a thaw and a new frost, there's not a sign to be seen. Nothing, anyway, that I can distinguish from the spoor of about a hundred coppers mooning around until told to stop. Come on.'

From the ditch, Keith retrieved an old fertilizer bag of white plastic. It was his habit to carry a sharp knife in a sheath taped across the back of his belt. He cut the bag into small squares before advancing into the field. 'There's no sign of whoever put the decoys out,' he said. 'The ground was frozen at the time. But the copper who picked up the decoys during the short thaw left his hoofprints behind. What do you see?'

'Just a ploughed field,' Mr Enterkin said dismally. He was not enjoying himself.

'Use your eyes and your sense. For a start, what would pigeon be looking for on plough? And the frost was too hard to get sticks in, so he wouldn't even be able to make them look convincing. But look where the bobby stopped and turned. There was one here . . . and here . . .' Keith placed his squares of white plastic in place, following the footsteps which the policeman had left the day before. 'Eighteen,' he said at last. 'I think that's the lot. And that looks like the pattern I saw from Munro's car. Too neat and round and tight. I never saw pigeon flock that way, and I can't believe they'd come in to decoys set out here like that. They might come over for a look, I suppose.'

'He did shoot some,' Mr Enterkin pointed out.

'But did he shoot them here? He could have been moved.'

'Moved?'

'Yes, of course. It was never likely that he was killed here.'

'Why on earth should anybody move him?'

58

'It's a bit early for guesswork, but I'll try one out for size. There was a racing pigeon in the bag. I thought it was feral because there wasn't a ring on its leg. But let's suppose that he's set up near somebody's loft. He kills somebody's racer, perhaps a very valuable bird. The owner sees it happen. There's a quarrel and a fight, and, next thing, Mr Muir's lying dead. "Oh dearie me," thinks the pigeon fancier, or words to that effect, "I can't have him found around here." So he loads the body and all the gear into the Land Rover and drives down this way. To save time he may fire up the Land Rover where it is and be setting up the decoys at this end while the police are already at the scene of the fire.'

'You think that's what happened?'

'I think there's about one chance in fifty. But if, for the racing pigeon, you substitute a bad debt, a pregnant daughter, an insult or any one of a dozen reasons why men quarrel, then I think there's a good chance I'm not far off.'

'Why set fire to the Land Rover?' Mr Enterkin asked keenly.

'Perhaps in the hope of passing it off as an accident. But just as likely because there was some clue on the body which had to be destroyed. Your guess is as good as mine. Well, not quite as good. You notice that there aren't any feathers lying around.'

'Should there be?'

'Pigeon feathers are very loose.' Keith took a last look around. 'Come on. We've seen all there is to see here.'

'Thank God!' Standing around in a freezing field was palling on Mr Enterkin. He headed back towards the farm road.

'Hold your horses,' Keith said. (Mr Enterkin halted with one foot in the air.) 'We'll walk from here to where the Land Rover was and see what we can pick up.'

'The police will have picked up anything of significance,' Mr Enterkin said with a sniff.

'If they knew it was significant. I've seen them find what they thought they were looking for and leave the rest. If you're too cold or too clapped-out, you can wait in the car until I come back.'

'I'd never hear the last of it if I did.' Mr Enterkin blew his nose violently into a large handkerchief. 'You always led me to believe that fresh air was beneficial, but it's giving be a cold.'

'You won't find any germs out here,' Keith said. 'The trouble is that you wrap yourself up like an eskimo and get your blood all heated while your sinuses are exposed to the frosty air. They aren't acclimatized yet. It'll pass.'

'It'd better or I'll sue you,' Mr Enterkin said.

They set off within the trees, each taking half the width and zigzagging to cover the ground. Keith, who had some experience of investigation, had provided himself with a section of Ordnance Survey map and two large polythene bags, and was insistent that every non-natural find be collected and that the position of any find which was either recent or even marginally interesting be marked on his map.

Progress was necessarily slow, but at least they were usually close enough for conversation.

'Would there be people in these woods at night?' Mr Enterkin asked suddenly.

'Like who?'

'Courting couples?'

'At this time of year, they'd have to be desperate.'

'Poachers, then?'

Keith laughed. 'You have eyes but see not,' he said. His childhood had been devoid of religion, but Biblical knowledge had figured largely. 'On a shooting estate the woods might be fenced off, though maybe not beside the road. You don't want pheasants at the roadside. Pheasants love crushed acorns or beach nuts, so you get crushed pheasants.' There was a pause while Keith collected an empty cigar packet and marked the map. 'On a farm like this, where shooting takes a poor tenth place, cattle are allowed into the wood for shelter and because the fencing's shorter like that. So there's no undergrowth. So there's nothing to poach.'

'So the Land Rover could sit there all night without being seen?'

'I should think so. You think it might have been there since the day before?'

Mr Enterkin stooped for a crisp bag and waited to regain his breath. 'I leave the thinking to you,' he said.

After more than an hour they came to the fence at which the police believed murder to have been committed. There was little to be seen except for the signs which the police themselves had left, just a spot of blood on a fence post.

They moved on. The field beyond the edge of the trees was now grass instead of plough. Keith pointed out where pigeon-droppings began. 'It'd've made more sense if the decoys had been put down in the nearest bit of field to the Land Rover,' he said. 'Why hump all the gear a mile away, and near to where they might be seen by the farmer?'

Mr Enterkin shrugged and snorted into his handkerchief.

'Well, think about it,' Keith said. 'If things look bad for Jake, we may need a complete alternative story which holds water. I must take a look down that way.' He pointed towards Newton Lauder. 'If Muir parked his Land Rover here, and was shooting further south, and somebody killed him in a place he didn't want the body found, it might make sense to leave the Land Rover where it was but to move the decoy site to the north. You follow me?'

'With igreasig difficulty,' Mr Enterkin said.

The Land Rover had been removed. Even the fragments which had been thrown among the trees were gone. While Mr Enterkin, with occasional ostentatious trumpetings into his handkerchief, sat on the same boulder where Keith had sat the day before, Keith scouted around. Here, at least, the police had been very thorough.

'I hope we've foud subthig worth all the effort,' Mr Enterkin said when Keith rejoined him.

'So do I. But at least when we know more we can see whether we've found anything to back it up.'

They were interrupted by the sound of a car followed by the arrival, on foot, of two men. Keith's first impulse was to put them down as a pair of nosey parkers, but he recognized the professionalism of the photographic gear slung from the stooping shoulders of the older man and guessed that they were a reporter with photographer in tow.

The reporter might have been thirty, but he had the sort of face which could have passed for sixteen. He was trying to give himself a mature image by cultivating a straggly beard, without any great success. He nodded in greeting. 'This is the third place we've tried to find where the man died in the burning Land Rover,' he said cheerfully. 'Is third time really lucky?'

Mr Enterkin tried again to clear his nose. 'This is the place where the burdig Lad Rover was foud, with a dead bad iddside.'

'We're from the *Edinburgh Herald*. And you are. . . ?'

'Dud of your dab busidess!'

'Hold on a moment,' Keith said quietly to Mr Enterkin. He faced the reporter. 'How much do you know?' he asked.

The young man hesitated and then shrugged. 'Not a lot,' he said. 'An amateur brought us in a photograph yesterday afternoon, but the locals already had it so we didn't follow it up. This morning we got a tip that there'd been an arrest. Even then, our editor was going to wait for the agencies. But our science correspondent recognized the name, Jacob Paterson, and said that he was a big-time inventor. So God sent us out to see what's going on. The police aren't saying anything yet, and when they do it'll be the barest bones. So what's the story?'

'We're looking around on behalf of Mr Paterson,' Keith said. 'You'll understand that we can't make any statements. But if your photographic colleague will give us a little help, we can give you a run-down on the physical facts as far as they're known and promise you first crack at anything we're prepared to give out later.'

The reporter had been eyeing Keith. 'I know you,' he said suddenly. 'I've seen you give evidence. You do the expert witness bit quite often, don't you? Can't either of you say anything useful?'

'Odely that our cliedt is cobpletely . . .' Mr Enterkin balked at the word innocent '. . . guiltless,' he finished.

'Solicitor for the defence,' Keith explained.

'Give me a quote, any kind of a quote, and Charlie'll help you out.'

'You couldn't use it,' Keith said. 'The case is . . .'

'*Sub judice,*' Mr Enterkin said.

'So you'd do better going to see the weeping widow. Anyway, the case may fizzle out into a non-event. On the other hand, it may turn into a *cause célèbre*—' (Keith was happier in French than in Latin) '—and if you help us out it's almost certain that your photographs will be introduced as evidence, and you'll already have them on file.'

'We could photograph this place for ourselves.'

'And my wife's a competent photographer,' Keith said. 'I can fetch her along to photograph the other place I have in mind.'

The reporter made a gesture of capitulation.

'Thirty-five mil do?' Charlie asked. In contrast to his colleague, he was an elderly man striving to look young, complete with Mexican moustache and contemporary clothes.

'Just so long as they're sharp,' Keith said.

63

'They'll be sharp.'

'I do't doe what you wad photographs for,' Mr Enterkin said. 'The police have picked the place clead.'

'At least we can show that they removed every scrap of evidence,' Keith said, 'so making it impossible for us to get anywhere with our own enquiries.'

Mr Enterkin nodded, reluctantly.

Keith directed operations as Charlie recorded what was left of the scene, including detailed shots of charred bushes and blast damage.

'Fidished?' Mr Enterkin asked.

'There's another site,' Keith told the reporter, 'where it will probably be suggested that the dead man had been shooting pigeon that morning. Our car's still along there. Give us a lift?'

'Surely.'

'Thag God!' Mr Enterkin said. He rose to his feet with an audible creak.

They squeezed into a rusting Beetle and puttered back towards the farm. Mr Enterkin reluctantly prepared to emerge again into the cold air.

'You could walk up to the farm while I see to the photographs,' Keith suggested.

Mr Enterkin shook his head violently. 'I'll cub back adudder tibe,' he said. 'I should be hobe id by bed.'

'I want to be back in Newton Lauder,' the reporter said, 'just in case the police make history by saying something interesting. I'll lift you there if Mr . . . Calder, isn't it? . . . if Mr Calder brings Charlie along when they've finished.'

Mr Enterkin subsided gratefully back into his seat.

FIVE

Keith and Mr Enterkin were both very busy for the next few days. In addition, the solicitor was aiding his own recovery by total avoidance of fresh air. Although they had spoken together on the phone, they did not meet again until they were due to visit Jake Paterson together in the headquarters building of the police in Newton Lauder. During the intervening days, Jake had made a brief appearance before the sheriff, at which no evidence was given and no application made for legal aid. He was remanded in custody for trial on a date to be set later.

The two men entered the old building which fronted onto the square, but were passed through into the bowels of the extension which towered over the original building and into a bare interview room. Within a few minutes Jake Paterson was brought to join them, but almost immediately Mr Enterkin was at the door and demanding to be directed towards a lavatory.

Jake and Keith seated themselves at a table which could have come from some works canteen, and met each other's eyes. Jake was slightly taller than Keith, and sturdier. He had inherited from his father a head of flaming red hair, and through his Jewish mother a nose which put into Keith's mind the thought that Jake would be regrettably easy for witnesses to describe.

Jake spoke first. 'This is a pretty kettle of fish,' he said with a crooked attempt at a smile.

'We can chat later,' Keith said. 'The reason Ralph Enterkin went for a pee is that he wants me to sound you out on things which he wouldn't want to hear from you direct.'

'I don't understand.'

'I'll try to explain. I've worked with Ralph before and I know how his mind works, so when he started hinting I got the message. If you were to say to him, "I strangled Fred Snooks with my bare hands," then, unless he could convince himself that you were lying, he'd feel debarred from briefing counsel to try and prove your innocence. But if you said the same to me, and then I told Ralph that I thought you might be guilty, he could still feel entitled to discount my opinion if there seemed to be a reasonable chance of getting you off. Fine shades of ethics, I know, but it's how the twisted legal mind works.'

Jake nodded slowly. 'For what it's worth, Keith, I did not do this thing.'

'I was sure of it,' Keith said. 'We both were. But you had to be asked. And now we need to know what it is that we've got to disprove. The most dangerous thing seems to be your relationship with the dead man's wife.'

'Oh, that!'

'Yes, that.' A new and unwelcome thought came to Keith. 'You don't think this place is bugged?'

For the first time, Jake looked amused. 'If it was, I'd have told you. I've been their consultant for the last seven or eight years, and if there was a bug in here I'd know it. And even if there were a bug, it wouldn't matter. The police haven't missed a trick.'

'They think you killed him for love of his wife?'

'They haven't been specific. They've suggested that motive, and also that we quarrelled because he decided not to invest in my new project after all. Neither supposition makes any sense, but if we disprove one of them they've always got the other to fall back on. I hadn't seen Neill Muir for more than a month. He was on his retirement leave, and he'd packed up his Land Rover and gone off to unwind. He had a thumping great golden handshake to come and we couldn't get started until it arrived, but he said that he'd be safe to spend his savings on a damn good holiday around the sporting hotels, picking up a day's shooting here and there.'

'And his wife didn't mind him taking off into the blue without her?' Keith asked. Molly would never have countenanced such a trip for himself unless he were accompanied by several companions, preferably ordained ministers, whom she knew she could trust.

'I don't know whether she minded or not,' Jake said, 'but she certainly wouldn't go along. He tried to interest her in the gentler side of shooting, but he said that it turned out to be her idea of hell.'

'And, contrariwise, he didn't mind leaving a sexy wife on her own while he went off?'

'I think he'd given up caring,' Jake said. 'And, frankly, I'd have done the same. That's why it's beyond reason for the police to imagine that I'd have killed in order to get her for myself for keeps. I'd have been more likely to kill to get rid of her. All right, so we were having a liaison, but it was strictly sex and no sentiment on either side. It was a lot of fun.' Jake lowered his voice. 'Between you and me, Keith, and any bugs that Munro may have sneaked in without my knowledge, between the sheets that woman is the most! But I wouldn't want her all to myself. I couldn't stand the strain. I'm not as young as I used to be. Demanding isn't the word for her.'

'What is?'

'I don't know. Voracious, perhaps. And self-centred. Outside of the bed, or inside it if her desires are satisfied for the moment, she's a bore. All she can think or talk about is herself and her woes. She's one of those people doomed to be permanently discontented. At the moment, she misses the big city.'

'Any particular big city?'

'I don't think so. She just feels that life out here among the cabbages is boring and primitive.'

Keith was about to ask whether the lady had seemed to regard her late husband as equally boring and primitive when the waiting constable opened the door. Mr Enterkin returned and took a seat at the table. He raised his eyebrows at Keith, who nodded.

'Jake admits to an affair with Mrs Muir,' Keith said. 'The police know. It wasn't serious.'

'Ah. And you are minding my counsel to restrain your tongue?' Now that his passages were again clear, Mr Enterkin seemed to enjoy using nasal consonants.

'I'm denying the murder and refusing to answer any questions,' Jake said.

'Good. Well, now that the matter of Mrs Muir is out in the open, tell us about it in as much detail as you think fit for general release.'

'I suppose so.' Jake paused, and Keith could have sworn that he detected a faint blush. 'I hope, more for her sake than mine, that this doesn't have to come out. Well, she picked me up in the hotel bar between two and three weeks ago.'

'She picked you up, and not the other way round?' Mr Enterkin asked.

'Call it mutual. But she was definitely on the prowl.'

'For you in particular, or just for a man?'

'Just for a man, I should think. She perched herself up on a bar stool, showing some delicious leg, twiddling an empty glass and smiling faintly at any man who made eye-contact with her. Well, my wife was somebody very special and since she died I've made no lasting contacts. But I have the same needs as the next man, and when I've been . . . without . . . for a period, temptation becomes very difficult to resist. When I bought her a drink, I had a pretty good idea of what I was in for. I just didn't expect quite so much of it,' Jake finished, smiling wryly.

'Did you know who she was?'

'Not at the time.' Jake turned and looked out of the window. They were four floors up and there were no bars. The view over the roofs of Newton Lauder to the hills beyond seemed to comfort him. 'She made no secret about being married but she never mentioned her married name. She said to call her Estelle.'

'That is her real name,' Mr Enterkin said.

'Is it? I'm surprised. Anyway, we used to meet at my flat because, although her husband seemed to be away a lot, husbands have been known to arrive home suddenly and without warning. Especially husbands of delicious blondes with roving eyes. I'd no wish to be like the lover in the old Glasgow joke, pushed out of the window with a shammy in my hand. I'd no compunction about the husband. If it hadn't been me it would have been some other unscrupulous sod.'

Mr Enterkin, whose marriage was recent and who still sometimes seemed to carry a faint whiff of orange-blossom, reminded himself that it was not for a lawyer to approve or disapprove of his clients. 'When did you find out who she was?' he asked.

Jake's shrug was a reminder of his mother's ancestry. 'Not until the morning of the murder,' he said. 'I've known one or two other wives who preferred to stay anonymous, so I just went along. She'd come to stay overnight on, I think, three previous occasions, always phoning first to say that she was coming. This time, she phoned the night before. Her husband was at home for the night but was going out early, so she fancied coming along for a morning frolic. I was none too keen, because I'd intended a morning foray against the woodies and I was leaving immediately afterwards for a holiday during which I wasn't exactly planning to stay celibate. But she was far too enjoyable to break with unnecessarily, so I said to come along early.

'She arrived at about seven-thirty, I suppose, because it

was just beginning to think about getting light outside. We – uh – exchanged several tokens of mutual esteem—'

'How many?' Keith asked.

'Mr Paterson's virility is not part of the *res gestae*,' Mr Enterkin said irritably. 'If it becomes so, then that will be time enough to explore the matter. Let us just accept that some time was spent in silken dalliance. How much time?'

'About an hour and a half,' Jake said. 'Longer than usual. She didn't usually dawdle, and I wanted to get away. But, just for once, she wanted to take her time. Then, when we were having a cup of tea and a cigarette and I was wondering how to coax her back into her clothes and away – because the pigeon would be on the move and I wasn't going to have much time to spare – she suddenly said that this was likely to be her last visit because she'd decided to leave her husband and go to live in Edinburgh. She said that her husband's retirement was now finalized. She'd hoped that he'd go with her, but he'd decided to stay around here and take a partnership in a local business. She said that she couldn't stick it out here in the wilds any longer. She made it sound like the Kalahari Desert.

'What she'd said sounded too much like Neill Muir for my peace of mind. So I asked her outright. She seemed surprised. She dithered a bit and then said yes, she was Mrs Muir.'

'The widow Muir, by then,' Keith said.

'Probably so. But we didn't know that. I was a bit stunned to realize that I'd been romping with the wife of the man who was going to put up half the capital for a new venture, but I decided that no harm had been done. He knew nothing about it, and she wasn't about to do something stupid like offering my name as a co-respondent. I could only thank my stars that she'd made it the last time.

'I got rid of her just after nine, expressing myself

heartbroken of course—'

'Of course,' Keith said. The courtesies have to be observed.

'I got in an hour at the pigeon and then headed south. They nailed me at Gatwick.'

'You two could alibi each other. But I gather,' Mr Enterkin said gently, 'that the lady claims to have been in her own bed at the time.'

'Does she know that I've been charged?'

'I'm afraid she must, unless her head's buried in the sand.'

Jake Paterson was silent for a minute, possibly, Keith thought, picturing Mrs Muir with her head buried in sand. Keith had not met the lady, as far as he knew, but even so he found the image intriguing.

'It's all right for her,' Jake said at last. 'She knows that she can fall back on me for an alibi if anyone should point the finger at her. She would only have to explain that she denied being with me for the sake of her reputation. If I claim that she was with me and she denies it, which she might do . . .'

'I would prefer that she stuck to her story,' Mr Enterkin said, 'but she won't. The police have a witness who can place her car below your flat that morning. Unfortunately, they know that I know it. Otherwise, that would have been a splendid weapon to smite the lady with in cross-examination. But the prosecution will see that danger.'

'Well, then.'

Mr Enterkin sighed. 'Don't refine too much on your chances of getting out of here on the lady's say-so. Although, as I said, you two could alibi each other, that will immediately be countered by the theory that either a timing device or a radio link was used. Conspiracy may be alleged. If not, for obvious reasons, you would be the more likely contender. Or is the widow Muir capable of constructing a remote-control device?'

'She could barely cope with a twisted bra-strap,' Jake

71

said.

'There you are, then. The alibi possibility will be followed up, but be prepared to learn that it is a snare and delusion.' Mr Enterkin looked at the ceiling and cracked his knuckles. 'Keith, your turn.'

Sometimes Jake was impelled by the impetuosity of his father's race, but now the gaze which he turned on Keith had the patience inherited from his Jewish mother.

Keith opened the folder in which he was accumulating such material as he could collect and which might contribute to Jake's defence. While he was finding his place, he asked idly, 'Why does the man Russell have his knife so deep into you? It's hardly your fault that he was wrong about your whatsit, and it's beyond reason to blame you for trying elsewhere after the British fuzz turned it down.'

'He told me what he thought of my ideas,' Jake said, 'and I told him what I thought of his mental ability.'

'His reaction suggests that you have the more pungent turn of phrase,' Mr Enterkin said. 'May that thought be a comfort to you in the weeks to come.'

Jake pulled a wry face and made one of his expressive shrugs.

'There are two areas I want to cover,' Keith said. 'The first one isn't very hopeful, but it's got to be tried. On the face of things, it looks as if Muir was out after the pigeon that morning also. But the place where his decoys were found was the last place I'd have chosen, and the setting-out didn't look very skilled. What's more, the farmer denies hearing any shots. There's a chance that the whole set-up had been moved, perhaps because the original place was a give-away to the real killer. So I've been traipsing around the hedgerows, looking for signs of decoying. Hides, feathers, empty cartridges and so on.'

Jake was visibly moved. 'Keith, I didn't know,' he said.

'Don't bother with that stuff,' Keith said gruffly. 'I dare

say there's half a chance you'd have done the same for me. Anyway, I've enjoyed it. It got me out of the shop. I've even collected a couple of hares. But the point is, I've pinpointed a dozen places. Most of them are fairly ancient, though, which fits in with the crop pattern. I mean, the old ones are beside last autumn's stubbles, which have been ploughed by now. Some of the others I've been able to eliminate. In fact, it's surprising how often I could identify the shooter from his habits, choice of cartridges and so on. The problem is that Muir could have gone twenty miles away, to some favourite spot we don't know about, and have fallen out with a local man, been killed and moved back nearer home. It's unlikely but it's possible, though the timing would be the tightest thing since Minnie the Midget lost her cherry. It might help if you told me where you were shooting.' He spread a map on the table. It was already marked and annotated with names familiar to Jake.

Jake turned the map round and took a few seconds to orient himself. Then he took Keith's pen and made a cross to the south of the town. 'Here,' he said.

'Ah. I hadn't got that far yet. And while I was out I didn't hear much from the south of me, just the occasional distant popping. There was somebody to the north of me, though. He fired three in quick succession, so unless there was two of him he had an automatic. I haven't found his site yet, though, so the tidy beggar probably picks up his empty shells. Charlie McLaren, do you think?'

Jake might not have the information which Keith gained through the shop, but he had happened upon most of the local pigeon men in the field at one time or another. He shook his head. 'He starts work early. So he's never out before work until later in the year. And Walter Wilson never picked up a spent cartridge in his life. Sounds to me like Watty Dunbar. He shoots on Brightside Farm.'

'Does Watty have an auto now?'

'He was carrying a Winchester pump-gun the last couple of times I bumped into him.'

'He didn't buy it from me. I'll ask him why when I follow him up.' Keith paused and made a note. 'Who did you hear, from where you were?'

'One man, firing two at a time. He was some distance away. I'd put him somewhere around Holly Wood.'

Keith made another note. 'If I can find him, and if he heard you, he might be useful. Not that he can alibi you for a time that seems to matter; but you never know. How many did you fire?'

'Ten or a dozen. I only got three. My reflexes were slow.'

'I bet. And then you drove to London at a hell of a lick. No wonder you got your head in a sling. You were using the old gun?'

Jaked nodded.

'In that case,' Keith said, 'he may have been able to identify you by the softer sound of your black-powder loads.' He finished his note and turned to a fresh page. 'You know about the explosion?'

'Only what Russell told me while trying to get me to admit to some unspecified activity in connection with it.'

Mr Enterkin cleared his throat. 'I've been unable to obtain sight of the forensic report. Munro's too nervous to meet me, or even to phone, but he sent his sergeant into the hotel last night on some quite spurious enquiry, and the sergeant mentioned, just by way of casual conversation, that – just as you said, Keith – traces of both gunpowder and modern smokeless powder were found, and in no small quantities.'

'Muir didn't reload his cartridges,' Keith said, 'so I can't see any reason for him to be in possession of two different sorts of propellant powders. The question is, Jake, how much of each ought there to be at your place?'

Jake's eyebrows shot up. 'You think that was mine?'

'Who else's?'

'Oh. I suppose it was slow of me not to have thought of it for myself. I suppose I ought to say "Oi vey!"?'

'Or "Begorrah!",' Keith suggested.

For the first time, Jake smiled. It was a thin smile and fleeting, but at least it was a smile. 'Consider them said. I stocked up at your shop. In fact, you served me yourself. About . . . two months ago?'

'About that.'

'As I remember it,' Jake said, 'I was down to about my last quarter-tin of each. I bought a half-kilo tin of Black Silver, and two half-kilo tins of Nobel Eighty. Since then I've loaded some skeet cartridges for using with my Browning over-under, because I was thinking of having a go at the Club competition next month, and a few black-powder cartridges. I haven't even finished the old tin of black powder, and I suppose I was about a quarter into the first of the new tins of Nobel.'

'So,' Keith said, scribbling, 'there should be at least a tin of the black stuff and nearly two of smokeless.' He looked up at the solicitor. 'Do we know how much was found at Jake's pad?'

'I'm afraid we do,' Mr Enterkin said. 'Penny reported the sergeant as remarking that no explosives were found. In my innocence I took it for good news. I take it that I was in a fool's paradise?'

'Correct,' Keith said. 'Jake, could Mrs Muir, on one of her visits, have made off with your tins and some of your empty cartridges? Or anybody else, of course.'

'Not from my flat,' Jake said. 'That's not where I kept them. My flat's only two rooms, and I like to keep it ready for visitors. There used to be a small room spare among the workshops behind my shop, so I took it over for gun work and loading.'

Keith was scowling down on his notes. 'But that's a high-

75

security area, right? You took me in there to show me the installation before you sold me my alarms. Who has the keys and the code? That overweight female who insults your customers for you?'

'She may be a bit on the flabby side,' Jake said gently, 'with overtones of superannuated Gaiety Girl. When it comes to dealing with customers, she may remind you of Genghis Khan in bloomers. She does me. But she's loyal and efficient, and she's the only person I'd trust to keep the business going while I'm in here. So I'll be even more grateful to you if you stop talking about her like that.'

'Sorry,' Keith said.

'And she doesn't have the keys and code to the private part of the workshops. Muir did, though.'

'He did?'

'Of course he did.' Jake sounded surprised that anyone could have thought otherwise. 'He was raising finance so that we could manufacture my radio-telephone and anything else which came along. He had to be able to demonstrate it to potential backers whether I was there or not. He had one of the units in the back of his Land Rover, but the main unit was in the workshop.'

'Oh, that's great,' Keith said dismally. 'That's just the ticket! So among the wreckage of the Land Rover they've found a whole lot of bits of radio receiver that didn't come out of a standard car radio. And in the workshop there's a matching transmitter which for all they know could have been up in your flat at the time. Right?'

'Almost,' Jake said. 'The main unit's big and it's bolted to the wall. Estelle – Mrs Muir – could hardly have missed seeing it if it had been up in the flat.'

'That's a relief. And, supposing the worst, if it wasn't there she couldn't describe it if she wanted to drop you in the clag.'

'Don't get too relieved,' Jake said. 'I ran a temporary cable from my flat to the workshop, so that I could turn a heater on about an hour before I went down to work there. It's a bit of a lash-up, but it serves its purpose. I could easily have used it to trigger a signal over the transmitter. And while Mrs Muir was there I noticed that I'd left the heater on overnight. So I threw the switch.'

'That's all we needed,' Keith said. 'That's just dandy!'

'That's dandy all right,' Jake said.

Preoccupied after his talk with Jake, Keith was hardly aware of the figure which crossed the square behind him. He was already speaking to Wallace by the time the man entered the shop, so Keith moved aside to let Wal serve the newcomer.

But the man produced a warrant-card and presented it to Keith. It identified him as Detective Chief Inspector James Russell. His manner was brusque, but there any resemblance to a Jack Russell terrier ended. (But, Keith remembered, the original Parson Russell's name was John.) Chief Inspector Russell was burly and carried himself so badly that his head seemed to be attached to the front of his deep chest rather than set on his shoulders. His nose was flattened, but his ears and lips were prominent, giving him the look of a clownish gargoyle. He was wearing a grubby sheepskin coat and a pork pie hat which remained firmly on his head.

'Mr Calder?'

With some reluctance, Keith admitted his identity. He had intended to ask Mr Enterkin for guidance as to what to say to the Edinburgh policeman, and he was regretting that this had slipped his mind. But, after years of association with the solicitor, he could almost hear his voice saying, 'Tell the truth but volunteer nothing.'

Russell produced a piece of paper. 'This is yours?'

The paper was one of the shop's receipts, made out to Jake in Keith's writing, for one tin of Black Silver and two tins of Nobel 80. 'This is ours,' Keith said.

'Under the Control of Explosives Act, you're required to

keep a record of all sales of gunpowder.'

This was a statement and as such, Keith felt, required no comment.

Russell's eyes narrowed. 'You have such a record?'

'We have.'

'Produce it.'

The policeman's manner had put Keith's back as far up as it could go. He was still wondering how to be most obstructive without laying himself open to prosecution when Wallace, behind the counter, produced the book from a drawer. Russell inspected it as if it had been composed of used toilet-paper. Jake's purchases were entered in Janet's neat hand.

'This is in a different writing,' Russell said. 'And it has been tampered with.'

Keith caught Wallace's eye. 'I can tell—' he began.

'I can speak for myself,' Wallace broke in. 'I'm Mr James, Mr Calder's partner. Mr Calder made the sale, but he was going out with Mr Paterson, so he asked me to enter the sale in the record.' Wallace showed Russell his right hand. Three fingers were missing. 'I don't write very well. I t-type most things, but book records have to be in manuscript. So I do them in pencil and my wife goes over them in ink, the same day.'

Russell drew himself up until his posture was almost normal. Keith could see him as he had been when he walked the beat, before desk work had affected his spine. 'At any time until Mrs James inks in your records, they could be falsified?'

'By whom?' Wallace asked.

'By you, for one.'

'I could have filled it in falsely in the first place,' Wallace pointed out.

'But,' Keith said, 'my receipt, the book record and the entry on Jake Paterson's Form F—which I filled out myself – all agree. Do you think we falsified the lot?'

'I'm making damn sure you didn't', Russell said. 'And ensuring that the law hasn't been broken.'

'Keeping a record in book form isn't law,' Keith said, 'it's only a piece of procedure demanded by the police, with powers you don't really have.'

Russell was studying the book. 'I wouldn't advise you to take that tone with me; I can turn nasty,' he said into its pages. He looked up and caught Keith's eye. 'Even nastier. You seem to have eight regular customers for black powder, including yourself and the prisoner Paterson. How many of the other six use their black powder to load cartridges?'

'How the hell would I know?' Keith said.

'You told Chief Inspector Munro that it was a common practice around here.'

'I don't think I said anything of the sort,' Keith said. 'You're putting words into my mouth. And if Munro inferred something like that from what I did say, I still didn't suggest that anybody doing so was necessarily my customer.'

Russell laid his finger on the page. 'These two lads, now. Isn't it true that each of these is a small contractor, who uses gunpowder occasionally to blast rocks or tree stumps?'

'I believe so.'

'To your knowledge, did either of them ever own a gun?'

'I don't know that they didn't,' Keith said.

'In other words, you don't know that they did. I can tell you that neither of them has ever held a shotgun certificate. The other four, now. Do you know for a fact that any one of them loads cartridges with gunpowder?'

Keith shook his head.

'On the other hand,' Russell said, 'isn't it true that you do know for a fact that each of them shoots a muzzle-loader? That you've sold each of them such a gun, or flints or percussion caps? And isn't it true that all four are members

79

of the Muzzle Loaders' Association, as you are also, and that you compete against them from time to time?'

Keith shrugged. Wallace decided to jump in. 'For all we know, any or all of them could load cartridges,' he said.

Russell ignored Wallace and spoke to Keith. 'What it amounts to is that, among your customers, the only users of black powder cartridges you know of are yourselves, Sir Peter Hay and the prisoner Paterson. True?'

'As far as we know,' Keith said, 'yes. But there's a lot more guns than that around here which have never been proved for smokeless powders.'

'How do you know? Did you sell them?'

'It'd be quite legal for me to do so,' Keith said. 'Proved is proved. But, in fact, whenever I get a gun traded in, or sold to me, which isn't proved for modern powder, I submit it for proof if I think it will pass. If I don't expect it to pass, I make it unusable and sell it as a wall-hanger. But there are a lot of them in service. I even get them in for servicing. Their owners may scrounge gunpowder cartridges, or they may buy their powder elsewhere.'

'Or they may just take a chance on their barrels standing up to the higher pressures generated by modern powders,' Russell said. 'Right?'

'That would be against the advice I always give them.'

'But people can be foolish?'

'You know it,' Keith said.

Russell lowered himself with a grunt into the customer's chair, leaving Keith standing over him. He smiled for the first time. His canine teeth were prominent and the smile suggested a snarl. 'There'll be somebody from the Procurator Fiscal's office coming to take a precognition from you. You will tell him just what you've told me – that as far as you know Paterson is the only person who buys gunpowder from you for the purpose of loading cartridges – or I shall come after you for every tiniest infringement I can dream up.'

'And if I qualify my statement?'

Russell's eyebrows went up. 'You *must* qualify it. It is just as important for the Advocate Depute to know what you might say if asked the wrong question.' (Keith nodded. He knew about precognitions and had already decided to reserve several points.) 'But you'll make these points clearly, and be prepared to speak to them if you're called as a witness for the prosecution. You load for yourselves and for Sir Peter Hay, but as far as you know Paterson is your only customer who loads his own. Not that I think we'll need you. I don't mind telling you that Forensic have already matched the firing-pin on Paterson's Westley Richards to the cartridges in Muir's bag. You were a bright boy there. Don't go and spoil it.'

He heaved himself to his feet and barged out of the shop.

'Phew!' Keith said.

'Not a n-nice man,' Wallace suggested mildly.

'Top of the Cops he is not. He heads my list of fuzz I would least like to be breathalysed by. I'll tell you this for nothing, Wal. Before this thing is over I'm going to do something unspeakably awful to that man.'

'Like what?'

'I don't know,' Keith said. 'I'll think of something. If God is good to me, I'll drop Detective Chief Inspector Russell so deep in the shit he'll never surface again. I wonder what Jake told him he was. Me, I don't know what he is. But whatever it is, he's the only one of it.'

Holly Wood was a rough plantation, mostly of sycamores but with some holly to justify its name, draped over a small knoll immediately south of the town. Only one corner of it adjoined land which could possibly have attracted pigeon, and here Keith found traces of a hide and the imprint of a round, five-gallon drum, presumably used both as a seat and as a gear-carrier. Keith could think of several men who used

81

this conveniently dual-purpose tool, and there were no other clues to the identity of the shooter.

So Keith approached the farmer, who gave him the names of three men with permission to shoot pigeon on that land. One of these, as Keith well knew, used a shooting-stick and another a folding canvas fishing-stool. He was unsure about the third, but tracked him down to a council house within sight of the wood.

He had found the right man. But the man had been shooting in a balaclava helmet with ear protectors over the top. These, together with the wind in the branches overhead, had prevented him from hearing anything.

Keith gave up, but stayed to chat for a few minutes about the shooting. He pricked up his ears when the man said that he had been using a flapper.

'How did you manage that?' Keith asked. 'Nobody else could get the peg into the ground because of the frost.'

'I've made an iron peg for mine. I can hammer it in. It didn't seem to draw the birds, though. For all the good I did pulling the string, I might just as well've been wanking myself.'

'You could have tied the string to your wrist and done both,' Keith pointed out.

SIX

By arrangement, Keith met Mr Enterkin next morning in the latter's dusty and cluttered office.

'I've tried to get hold of Watty Dunbar,' Keith said. 'But he's just gone out to do a job in the Persian Gulf. He's a welder-diver. I think you should send this cable.'

'Is it important?' Mr Enterkin asked.

'If I knew that, I wouldn't need to send it.'

Mr Enterkin took the paper from Keith. It read:

WALTER DUNBAR, C/O SUBAQUATECH, BAHRAIN.
WERE YOU ON BRIGHTSIDE FARM LAST TUESDAY MORNING QUERY PLEASE ADVISE URGENTEST ALSO PROBABLE RETURN DATE
ENTERKIN NEWTON LAUDER 4728

'Very well,' Mr Enterkin said. 'Give it to Miss Wilkes when you go.'

'I'll give it to her now,' Keith said. He left the room. In a few seconds he returned. 'She'll send it off straight away,' he reported.

'Why the hurry?'

'Because I'm grinding to a halt until I get a new lead.'

Mr Enterkin nodded. 'Then we must seek to open up new lines of enquiry,' he said. 'Tell me, could the explosion have been caused by an accident of some kind?'

'That depends.' Keith thought for a minute. 'Muir's gun wasn't found in the wreckage.'

The solicitor showed his customary sign of irritation. He looked slightly less cherubic than usual. 'Never mind the extraneous evidence,' he said. 'We can seek to explain any such discrepancies once we have a basic theory. In its own right, could the explosion have been an accident?'

'Easily, given one or two assumptions. One of the snags to gunpowder throughout history has been that if it gets bounced around, as in a vehicle, it can produce a very fine and very explosive dust.'

'Aha! So if Muir got into his Land Rover and lit a cigarette?'

'Did he smoke?'

'That is something we shall have to find out.' Mr Enterkin made a note. 'I never saw him smoking, to be sure. But even a man who does not smoke regularly might enjoy an occasional cigar. Or there are other possible reasons for striking a match. Admittedly, I can't think of one just at this moment—'

'Nor can I,' Keith said.

'—but the suggestion might be enough to set the jury thinking.'

'Is that a good idea? They might think too much. How did the dust get out of a tin with a screw cap?'

'If, as you suggest, it had been bouncing around in the back of the Land Rover, could the cap not have screwed itself off?'

'Just possibly. But then, if the lid wasn't on tight it wouldn't make much of an explosion. Propellant powders need to be confined if they're to make a real bang.'

'Ah,' Mr Enterkin said. He pouted in deep thought. 'But suppose, just suppose that the screw cap had come off the tin of gunpowder and the fine dust was loose in the Land Rover. Mr Muir gets in and for some reason not yet known he creates a naked light. The uncapped tin of gunpowder goes off right beside the two tins of smokeless powder which, again for some reason not yet known, he had borrowed from Mr Paterson's workroom. Would the tins of smokeless powder go off and, if so, would their explosion be sufficient to rupture the fuel tank of the Land Rover?'

'Yes to the first,' Keith said. 'As to the second, I think so. It isn't like the controlled explosion of a measured quantity of propellant at a calculated rate under known conditions, as in a cartridge in the chamber of a gun. Probably you wouldn't get quite the same results twice. If you cared to supply me with half a dozen Land Rovers . . .'

'A damned expensive way of finding out,' Mr Enterkin said, 'and fortunately beyond the means of the prosecution. But no!' The solicitor snapped his fingers in annoyance. 'What am I thinking about? The prosecution will prefer the assumption that the tins of explosive material in Mr Paterson's possession would be sufficient. It would be to our advantage to show that it would have taken a dozen tins of powder to have done so much damage.'

'Except that Jake could have bought the extra somewhere else,' Keith pointed out. 'Nitro powders can be bought freely. What beats me is why Muir should be carrying powders anyway. He didn't reload. He told me so.'

'He could have started since then,' Mr Enterkin said. 'Or intended to.' He made another note. 'He could have bought himself all the relevant materials elsewhere. Yours isn't the only gunshop within reach, you know. He could have stocked up with the materials while on his tour. After all, he was just entering on his retirement, which suggests a period of increased leisure and reduced affluence. Wouldn't that be a good time to start loading his own cartridges?'

'And the gunpowder?'

'Unless the prosecution has proof to the contrary, we can always suggest that he might have bought, on his travels, a gun which needed that kind of coddling. No doubt, with your customary ingenuity, you can oblige me with some theory which would allow for both guns being stolen from the vicinity of the Land Rover.'

'The police would have a record if Muir had been granted a Form F.' Keith pointed out.

'But if they've failed to do their homework, we can cloud the issues in court. With evidence so circumstantial – so far as we know for the moment – we only have to show that that evidence can be explained in other ways. And you know well, Keith, how easily Muir could have obtained a supply through a friend. Illegally but easily. He had friends?'

'I wouldn't know.'

'There is too much that we don't know,' Mr Enterkin said. 'And the police are being very sluggish about revealing anything which could be of use to the defence. The normal courtesies have gone by the board. I think it's time we paid a call on the weeping widow.'

'She is weeping, is she? Not singing and dancing?'

'She was weeping when I called on her that first morning, before the police sent me packing. Tears streaming down her face. I was not in much better shape myself. I trust that she will have recovered her composure by now. Nothing so much puts me off my food as a weeping woman. I have some experience – not in my marriage,' Mr Enterkin added hastily, 'but as a solicitor. Would you be free this evening? The lady seems to be spending her days in Edinburgh and only returning home overnight.'

'I think I'm free,' Keith said. 'Molly might not agree. I've been neglecting her, and Deborah's beginning to wonder who the funny man is.'

'Suppose I were to phone her and ask whether she could persuade you to help me out on Jake Paterson's behalf?'

'At last you're beginning to think like a married man,' Keith said.

Although Mr Enterkin kept a Rover 3000, it was his habit to drive, if he drove at all, very slowly. He drove not by habit and instinct but with constant thought and it made Keith nervous. But when Mr Enterkin called for him that evening Keith could not without causing offence suggest that they changed cars or that he take over the wheel. He trod on imaginary pedals while they followed the valley northwards.

The frost was holding. As they climbed, they left the salted and gritted roads and began to slip and slither on packed snow. The night was dark with only a thin sliver of moon, but Keith knew that the countryside also had changed. They were above the trees and the mixed arable farming of the lusher level. Here was sheep country, grass and heather.

Their road branched, became smaller and rougher. They passed a row of cottages and came at last to a small farmhouse, set down uncompromisingly where open moor began. The only other lights belonged to the row of cottages and to one other farmhouse a mile away. Otherwise, not even distant headlamps punctured the dark.

Mrs Muir must have heard the car stop in what was now no more than a lane. A lamp came on over the door, and as they walked across the yard a rhomboid of light widened across the frozen gravel. A female figure, evidently that of Mrs Muir, stood in silhouette, and for a moment Keith felt a pang of sympathy for Jake's frailty. She was perfectly proportioned. Her thorax and thighs, accented by a cat-suit grossly inappropriate for a frosty rural night, were two perfect ovals from which sprang other gentle curves. Her hair, shoulder length, glowed against the light. As she moved forward her face came under the overhead lamp, and even in that cruel light Keith could see that she had beauty, not of the severe, classical sort but of the kind which is seen in men's magazines. He wondered how anything like that could have walked the streets of Newton Lauder without his having been aware of it.

The lady's manners, it appeared, were not in the same class as her looks. 'What do you want?' she demanded of Mr Enterkin. 'I thought the will was dealt with.' She ignored

Keith altogether.

Mr Enterkin raised his hat. He was at his most suave. 'It is indeed,' he said. 'Everything's been delivered to the executor. But, as you may know, I'm acting as Mr Paterson's solicitor and I've come to ask you for a little help on his behalf.'

She jerked her head at Keith and raised her eyebrows. A ring flashed on her right hand as she made a small gesture.

'Mr Calder is doing some investigating for me,' Enterkin said. 'We hoped to ask you one or two questions and perhaps to take a look at where your late husband kept his guns.'

Mrs Muir looked at Mr Enterkin for a moment without disfavour. Keith thought that he could even detect faint gender-signals passing. Then her eyes flicked to himself and her nose went up. She turned her shoulder to him. 'Why should I help the man who killed my husband?'

Mr Enterkin tried not to sigh. Her question betrayed the attitude which is the bane of defence lawyers' lives. 'He has been charged,' he said, 'but surely he is entitled to a fair trial. We all want truth to prevail. Did your husband have many friends?'

'It's too bloody cold to stand out here,' she said, and indeed Keith could see that she was shivering. Mr Enterkin moved forward but she stood squarely in the doorway. 'No, you're not coming in. It's bad enough having to live alone at the arse-end of the world without being badgered by a lot of men.'

'And yet,' Mr Enterkin said, 'Mr Paterson must have meant something to you once. Tell me, did your husband have only the one gun, or did he buy another during his last trip?'

'I don't have to tell you a damn thing,' the lady said. 'I've been advised. You can wait to hear what I say in court. Or if you want to use me as a witness you can cite me, and the best of British luck.' She stepped back out of the overhead light.

'Have you confirmed Jake's alibi?' Keith asked quickly.

For the second time she looked down her nose at him. 'Do me a favour,' she said. 'No, three favours. Fuck off. Fuck right off. And stay fucked off.'

The door slammed.

They drove in silence for the first mile home, fuming.

Keith's indignation arose from hurt pride. Male pride. Like any good chauvinist he venerated women while still expecting to be allowed his superiority. Nor was he any kind of snob, real or inverted. Considerations of social status were never in his mind. He looked neither up nor down on duke or dustman. Once, while on holiday, noticing the existence of a self-styled 'in-crowd' he had thought the matter over and decided that they were not 'in' with himself and therefore could be of no importance. Because Keith gave or withheld his respect according to whether or not it had been earned, he naively expected others to do the same.

Mr Enterkin's chagrin rose from more practical considerations. 'That damned woman,' he burst out at last. 'Her lover – or possibly ex-lover – is standing trial for murder and she grudges us the least bit of help.'

'Couldn't you ask the court to order her co-operation?' Keith asked.

'A statement taken under those circumstances is regarded by the witness as a sort of rape,' the solicitor said, 'and is usually about as satisfying. We could ask for an order to admit us to the premises for a search, but in view of the fact that there is no allegation of a crime having been committed there and that we can't specify what we expect to find, it might all take time which we haven't got.'

'Why the hurry?'

'Because she has already found the flat in Edinburgh which she wants to buy, and is placing her own house on the market. Hence her concern over expeditious handling of her husband's will, of course.'

'Surely,' Keith said, 'she wouldn't be allowed to move house just now?'

'Why not? As far as the police are concerned, the house and its contents are irrelevant. I'll try the sheriff straight away, of course. But if the police, or the fiscal's office, suggest that this is mere harassment of a poor, grieving widow. . . .'

'At the least, we've got to see inside,' Keith said. 'We can't have her moving house and chucking out or giving away just the sort of junk we'd be interested in.'

There was a pause while the solicitor braked and turned with great care into the by-road which served Briesland House. 'I would be doing less than my duty,' he said suddenly, 'if I failed to warn you that under no circumstances must you contemplate entering that house.'

'I wouldn't dream of doing such a thing. Could you get me in to see Jake tomorrow? There's something I want to ask him.'

'I suppose that it is not a question which I could ask on your behalf?'

'No,' Keith said, 'it isn't.'

'Come and see me in the morning.' Mr Enterkin braked to a halt outside Keith's front door and sat looking through the windscreen. 'I know you wouldn't dream of entering that house,' he said, 'so I need hardly bother to point out that, in the event of your doing so, any signs of illegal entry would invalidate such evidence as you might find; nor that, in the event of your finding anything, it must on no account be abstracted. Once removed from its context its value as evidence would be destroyed, whereas mere knowledge of its existence can be invaluable. I can almost hear counsel's voice. "Remember, Mrs Muir, you are on oath. Is it not true that you have in your possession, among your late husband's chattels . . ." And so on and so forth.'

Mr Enterkin, when Keith reached his office the next day, was studying and annotating a newly arrived cable. 'Mr Dunbar,' he said, 'seems to have received our cable and even to have understood it, which is little short of a miracle if it passed through the same channels as his reply. Channels which seem to be imperfectly acquainted with this or any other language. I will not bore you with a precise rendition of what seems to have been translated literally into some debased Arabic dialect and back again, and to have been seriously garbled in the process. I need only say that, in the unlikely event that I am reading him aright, Mr Dunbar would indeed have been out after the pigeon early that day, because he did so every morning for a fortnight prior to his departure. But he is uncertain as to the details of that particular day. He suggests that we, which means you, should obtain his game-book, whatever that might be, from his mother and cable him any relevant details, whereupon he will endeavour to answer our questions. I sincerely trust that his information is going to justify the expense.'

'I hope so,' Keith said. 'The cost of cables is soon going to overtake your fee.'

'I wouldn't say that,' Mr Enterkin said with satisfaction. 'No, I wouldn't go that far for a moment. Well, come along, my boy. We'll pay our call on the unfortunate Jake.'

They were reunited with Jake Paterson in the same interview room as before, and Mr Enterkin immediately repeated his request for the toilet.

Jake, Keith noticed, had lost weight.

'While we're alone,' Keith said, 'tell me this. You installed the alarms at the Muirs' house?'

'That's right.'

'You did it personally?'

Jake nodded. 'That's the one bit of the business I see to entirely myself. I'd like to trust my employees; but you can't be too careful when a dishonest employee could do the firm so much damage. While I'm in here, that work will just have to hang fire. I gave Muir the same installation you've got.'

'Do you,' Keith asked casually, 'happen to remember what code it was set to?'

Jake jumped as if one of his own computers had goosed him. 'You're not thinking of burgling the woman?' he said.

'There's information we must have, and she's being as obstructive as she can get. She's acting as if she wants to see you jugged.'

'She confirmed my alibi, for what it's worth.'

'For what it's worth,' Keith agreed. 'And she confirmed her own at the same time. And she's planning to move house. In all innocence, she could throw out the very clues which might clear you.'

'You'd be putting your head on the block.'

'You'd do the same for me.'

'You said that once before,' Jake reminded him. 'But that time we weren't talking about you taking a few pleasant country strolls. This time, we're talking about you taking a chance on joining me in here. And I'm not sure that I would do that much, even for a friend, so don't go counting on it.' Jake paused, and gave his expressive shrug. 'I don't want to talk you out of risking your all for me.'

'You couldn't,' Keith said. 'But you could make it less of a risk.'

'I wish I could, but I don't think I can. When I put the system in, I left it set to be cancelled by the sequence one-two-three-four, on Muir's own instructions, and showed him how to re-set the code for himself.'

Keith looked at his watch. Time might be running short before Mr Enterkin's return cut off this line of discussion. 'Could I silence it from outside?' he asked.

Jake raised his eyes to the ceiling. 'If you could, you'd want your own money back. I couldn't do it myself. Not without it yodelling for ten seconds or more.'

Keith made a face. He knew that electronic yodel. It was designed to wake the dead; and the Presbyterian minister, who had a dry humour, had once suggested that such devices should be banned within a mile of a burial ground, to save wasted effort. 'If I go in the front door . . .' Keith said.

'Then you've got two minutes to punch the right code. And if you punch one wrong digit it'll go off. Dammit, Keith, it's designed to be impossible.'

'In that case, old friend,' Keith said, 'there's a high chance you'll go up the river.'

'That's different,' Jake said. 'Let me think.'

Mrs Dunbar, mother of the expatriate Watty, was a plain, plump widow with a twinkle in her eye and a sparkle in the small villa which she occupied on the outskirts of the town. She invited Keith into her parlour, all rosewood and plush and china, and gave him coffee and chocolate cake with cream. It was the first tenet of her beliefs that men needed feeding. Keith could well understand why Watty Dunbar would flee to the Middle East to lose weight – and then make tracks for home again.

'Watty's mentioned your name,' she said.

'I'll bet he said that I'm expensive but usually worth it. That's what he told me, once.'

'Oh, not about the shop. He said he could sometimes shoot as well as you do, but he wished he could do it a' the time.'

'He could, if he kept his mind on it.' Keith showed her her son's cable. She fetched the game-book and left him alone while he copied out the entry for the crucial morning. This was in diary form.

November -th.
Out v. early. Bright dawn, v. cold wind off hill. Took S.E. corner of Hallerton Wood shooting over kale. Ground too

hard for sticks, decoys not life-like and flapper impossible.
Lofter helped draw birds from south. Company later.

Woodpigeon	8 }	over kale
Collared doves	3 }	
Mavis	2	over straw
Cartridges	18	(No 6 reloads)

Winchester 12g with ½-choke.

Mrs Dunbar returned while Keith was glancing back through the book. She brought with her a large glass of beer. 'Watty's got you well trained,' Keith remarked.

'I like fine to have a man to look after,' she said.

'Watty seems to fancy the Hallerton area. He could've got more birds nearer home.'

'I doubt Hallerton has its attractions,' she said. 'And I'd not want him bringing home even more cushie-doos. The freezer's about full of them already. It's usually duck he's after, but they tell me there's a ban.'

An hour later, when Keith showed Mr Enterkin his notes, the latter seemed unimpressed. 'I can cable the information out to Mr Dunbar,' he said, 'and hope that it'll jog his memory.'

'I think it will.'

'The mavis is the common thrush, isn't it?'

'Yes. You might add that Calder wants to know whether his brace of *Turdus philomelos* was a right-and-left.'

The solicitor looked puzzled. 'If I'm correct in my interpretation of all the technical jargon with which you've been bombarding me,' he said, 'Dunbar was using a gun which had but the one barrel. How then could he have scored a "right-and-left"?'

'Just ask the question,' Keith said, 'and we'll see what he says.'

'Very well. I'm told,' Mr Enterkin said, looking anywhere but at Keith, 'that Mrs Muir had to miss her Edinburgh trip today, although why that should be of any interest to you evades me. Apparently there was a surveyor coming out to see the house. And Penny assures me – and again I can think of no reason for telling you this – that when Mrs Muir does not go to Edinburgh it is her custom to visit Newton Lauder in the evening in search of male companionship.'

'You think that she might take a shine to me?' Keith asked.

'You never know your luck,' Mr Enterkin said. 'After all, she might be in the mood for a bit of what I believe is known as "rough".'

SEVEN

That same evening, long after dark, Keith drove up the hill behind the Town Hall to collect his brother-in-law, Ronnie Fiddler. Molly's brother was a large, rough-hewn individual of uncertain temper and, in Keith's view, no very great intelligence. At the moment they were friends, so good that Ronnie was quite prepared to risk prosecution when Keith asked it of him. The fact that Keith stood well enough with Ronnie's employer to smooth over any resulting absences may have helped.

They drove past the Muir house, where the presence of the red hatchback suggested that Mrs Muir had not yet left for her evening's dalliance, and on up the valley. The road deteriorated into a track. Keith turned at a gate and freewheeled back down the road, lit only by the palest of moonlight and by his sidelights wherever he was sure that they could not be seen from the house. He parked where a dry-stone wall would hide most of the car but from where he could see Mrs Muir's front door.

Ronnie had, after his fashion, been thinking. 'A woman like her,' he said, 'with her looks, she'll have no trouble scoring with a bloke. She could be back here before we're out.'

'They're not all as quick as you are,' Keith said. 'Some people take upwards of twenty minutes.'

'I don't hang about,' Ronnie said complacently.

'Anyway, I've got Wal primed. He wanted to pour a couple of buckets of water over her car. But I said that'd be too obvious. An eye-dropper of water in each of the door locks should be enough in this frost.'

96

'Some interfering idiot'll come out with a blowlamp,' Ronnie said.

'It all takes time.'

'Or the man could run her home.'

'That's the danger. That's mostly why you're along, to keep watch and to be a witness . . . mostly to bear me out that we never went inside the place at all.'

'Oh, I can do that all right,' Ronnie said.

They settled down to wait. Keith played a Bach cassette. Ronnie moved restlessly in his seat. His taste favoured Jimmy Shand rather than Johann Sebastian. 'How are you going to get us in? If the system's the same as yours, the infra-red thingies'll have you pegged in a jiffy.'

The ploy worked. Keith turned the music down to a whisper. 'It'll have to be the front door,' he said. 'That way I've got two minutes before all hell's let loose. There's no way I can kill the system before it sounds off, but if I'm quick enough I can fix it before it lets off more than one or two whoopees. But it does that sometimes when you're setting or unsetting it or when there's a hiccup in the electrical supply, so I doubt if the neighbours will stir.'

'You can do it in about a second? If it yelps more than twice, I'm out and running.'

'You'll stay put or else,' Keith said. 'I need you. Once I've opened the front of the box, I've got problems. If it is unset, I'll only have to push in the hidden latch which the lid usually holds in, but set it's going to sound off until it's given the code.' Keith was thinking aloud, reminding himself of Jake's instructions. 'You've seen the thing. There's four numbered buttons on the front, which have to be touched in the right sequence. When you open the thing, you can see four flexible wires connecting the terminals behind the buttons to four other terminals marked A to D and that's the order they've got to be pressed in. If you had time you could look and see which button was connected to A and press it

97

first, and so on.'

'Aye,' Ronnie said. 'If.'

'Jake thinks that earthing the terminals, from A to D, would do the same job.'

'Thinks?'

'I tried it on my set-up and it worked. So the drill's this. We go in. I've got a wire in my pocket, and we earth the end of it. I drop the front of the box, pass the end of the wire across the terminals and hold the latch in. You pull the four wires off their terminals, but keep them so that we can put them back the way they were. Got it?'

''Course. What about the door. Going to slip it with your credit card?'

'You've been reading too many thrillers,' Keith said. 'You can't do that to a door that opens inwards. The stop's in the way.'

'Then how—?'

'You'll see. If it works.' Keith turned the volume up again. The car grew colder. Ronnie sat and suffered until, just as he was about to suggest that they gave it up for the night, the front door light came on and Mrs Muir, cosily furred, hurried into her car and drove off.

'Come out this side and try not to leave footprints,' Keith said. He lifted a bundle off the back seat. They walked softly, breathing out steam. The frost was bitter.

'The bitch has left her front door light on,' Ronnie whispered.

'I don't think you can see the front door from the cottages. Not from downstairs anyway. This time of night, they'll be in front of their tellies.'

'I bloody well hope so.'

They reached Mrs Muir's door. 'I see what you mean,' Ronnie said.

'Let's not hang about.' Keith opened his bundle. It contained three pieces of wood of assorted lengths and a car

98

jack. He found the appropriate length. 'Hold this here and that there,' he said. Within a few seconds he had the jack and one piece of wood braced across the doorway between his two other timbers, and as he pumped the jack handle the doorposts were forced apart. They creaked. Keith stopped.

Ronnie tapped the glass beside the door. 'This'll break if you go on.'

Keith nodded. 'The frame's twisting. I can get a card in now.' He worked a piece of flexible plastic into the gap. There was a click. He caught the door before it could move more than half an inch. 'Get the jack out and wrap the bundle up again. Bring it in with you and shut the door behind us. We want the cloakroom just inside on the left. Follow me in fast and hold the torch for me. Ready?'

'Right.'

'Geronimo!' Keith whispered. He pushed the door open and the buzzer sounded its low, warning note. He flashed the torch. The first door on his left led into a cloakroom-cum-lavatory. His heart almost stopped when he failed to see the control box. But there was a cupboard over the basin with a mirrored door. He snatched it open, and the box winked at him with its little coloured eyes, comfortably familiar.

The buzzer droned on. His time was leaking away.

The pipes under the basin were chromed. That should do. He twisted a bared end of his wire around a pipe. Ronnie was by his side, and he handed over the torch and got to work with his pocket screwdriver, holding the end of the wire between his teeth. He dropped the two screws into the basin after putting in the plug.

'Ready?'

'Aye.'

'Go!'

He let the front of the box drop on its hinges. The alarm outside squealed like a terrified cuckoo. Keith stabbed at the latch with his left forefinger while with his right hand he

99

swept the free end of his wire across the terminals. Ronnie's big hand came over his shoulder and jerked at the four little wires. Silence returned, dropping like a huge, fleecy blanket.

'No' bad,' Ronnie said. 'Three yodels at the most. We'll have to take this up.'

'My left jacket pocket. A roll of sticky tape. Take me off about three inches.'

With the latch – a pressure-switch – taped, Keith relaxed. 'Now, gloves on,' he said, 'and we'll take a look around. Just a moment.' He looked into the box again. 'Where are the four little wires?'

'Here.' Ronnie displayed them in his broad palm.

'How am I supposed to put them back the right way?'

'I don't bloody know,' Ronnie said plaintively. 'You just said to keep them.'

There was nothing to be gained by argument. Keith had a rough mental picture of how he thought the wires had been. He filed it away for future use. 'Ten to one I can't put it back the way it was,' he said. 'I'd rather she didn't know she'd been visited.'

'What happens if that bittie tape slips?'

'We run like hell.'

From the front door, no sign of neighbourly curiosity could be seen. Across the wide hall from the cloakroom, double doors stood open to a sitting-room. Even by torchlight it was seen to be furnished in good taste and at some expense. The red eye of an infra-red sensor winked on as they looked in. A log smouldered in the grate.

'What'll happen wi' the alarms?' Ronnie asked.

'If I don't guess right, first time she tries to unset the alarm all hell will break loose. And there's no way she can stop it without expert help. The best she'll be able to do will be to get an electrician to pull the fuse and wait a couple of hours for the batteries in the outdoor unit to run down. Or send for the installer, who's in pokey. If she wants it working again, she'll have to send for somebody from Edinburgh or Newcastle. Come on.'

The late Mr Muir's study was at the back of the house. Another red eye came on as they entered. Keith drew the curtains. 'We should be safe enough, this side of the house,' he said, and switched on the lights.

The room seemed to have been left undisturbed since its master's death. The layout reflected his different activities. The side on their right, with the window, was given over to paperwork, with a desk and several filing cabinets, all very neat and orderly. To the left was a workbench, less tidy, with shelves above which were jumbled with odds and ends. On the far wall was a large wardrobe, battered relic of some Victorian household but now, Keith found, demoted to a repository for shooting clothes and the larger items of gear. A camouflage net was stuffed into the bottom over several pairs of boots, and on a shelf Keith saw the green-painted wire frame for a flapping decoy.

'None of this means much,' he said. 'Without the widow's co-operation, we don't know what he had duplicates of.' He transferred his attention to the workbench side of the room. 'No reloading,' he said. 'And no sign of muzzle-loaders.'

'A one-gun man,' Ronnie added. 'Kept it on they two pegs.'

The bench itself was old, battered and scarred and showing the occasional burn. The few tools were not solely for gun maintenance, and the shelves were cluttered with the odds and ends which accumulate around a not very handy householder. Keith's eye passed contemptuously over the few screwdrivers, a hammer, a hand drill and a hacksaw with broken blade. The equipment for basic gun-cleaning was there – tins and aerosols of gun oil, wax for a gunstock, cloths, a patent barrel-cleaner and a cleaning rod with a bronze wire jag. The boxes of cartridges were tidily arranged. Keith guessed that Mr Muir had favoured 7s and

8s for clay pigeons. The 6s would have been for woodpigeon and general game, 3s for duck and the BB definitely for geese. Mr Muir had liked his shot on the heavy side.

'Look at this,' Ronnie said suddenly. His gloved hand lifted a shape of steel and walnut off the lower shelf. 'The fore-end of a gun.'

Keith studied the find carefully. 'When I met Neill Muir, he was carrying a Sabel de Luxe. This could belong to it. Or,' he added, 'this could be off some gun that was lost or stolen or damaged and scrapped. Put it back carefully, on its side so that you can see the number from the window. And hand me down that box.'

The box, which had once held half a gallon of ice-cream, now contained those small oddments which are kept 'just in case ' – screws and hinges, tap washers, a padlock, a broken window-catch. Keith was about to return it to the shelf when he paused at a small ring which might have been cut from the leg of a racing pigeon. Just on the off-chance he copied the number into his notebook beneath the number of the fore-end and put the ring beside the fore-end on its shelf. The box he restored to the shelf above, and then he stood, brushing crumbs of wax off his gloved finger-tips and looking around.

'There's no sign or smell of him ever having smoked,' he said. 'Which makes it more difficult to put forward an accident theory. Come on. We'll take a quick look at the rest of the house.'

Time can pass quickly when one is enjoying oneself, and Keith, if pressed, would have had to admit that he enjoyed his trip through a strange house, building up a picture of a couple whose ways were alien to him. Outside of the study, there was no doubt that what Mrs Muir had wanted she had obtained; or else every trace of her husband's wishes had been expunged with remarkable speed.

Keith had allowed himself an hour from entering the

house. He guessed that, in the days when he was young and predatory, that would have been the shortest time ever to have elapsed between his setting out on the prowl and returning to his chosen love-nest with compliant company. But his watch, when he looked at it, announced that an hour and a half had gone by. They did one quick tour to ensure that all was apparently as they had found it and made for the cloakroom.

Except that Keith had to reset the code by memory and guesswork, they reversed exactly the procedures which they had followed on entry. As Ronnie removed his hand, Keith slammed the lid and punched the new code. The alarm had time for no more than a single yip.

The two men breathed more easily.

And then, as Keith picked up the screws, one of them slipped from his fingers and tinkled across the tiled floor. He stood, leaning against the box. 'Find it, for Christ's sake,' he said.

'Can I put the light on?'

'No way. This window must look right down the valley. Take the torch.'

While he waited, Keith fumbled the other screw into place, very carefully, with his spare hand.

'Got it!' came Ronnie's voice at last. As he pushed the screw between Keith's fingers, a car door slammed outside.

The torch went out.

'Put it *on*.' Keith grabbed the torch and screwed one-handed. The screw ran in. Was there a chance of getting to the back door?

There was not.

As Keith made time for a quick wipe over the face of the box with his sleeve, the latch of the front door clicked and the door let a cold draught find its way to the cloakroom window by way of the small of Keith's back. He snapped off the torch, picked up his bundle and stepped to where the cloakroom door might screen him if it opened. Bright light fanned across from under the door.

'That's funny,' said Mrs Muir's voice. The lack of the warning tone had caught her attention. 'I could have sworn I set the alarms.' Her voice was richly unconcerned. Other things were on the widow's mind. The cloakroom door opened and the light came on. There was no sign of Ronnie. Keith could smell her perfume, even see the edge of her skirt through the crack of the door. 'There must be another damn fault,' her voice said. 'Well, if you're supposed to be some sort of electrician, you can take a look at it for me before you go.' The door closed. The light died.

Hugging his bundle to his chest, Keith breathed deeply. He heard muffled voices, the clink of glasses. Erotic music throbbed softly and he wondered in passing where he could buy the tape. It seemed to have something. Otherwise all was silent. Where the hell were they?

After an eternity without change Keith turned the handle and eased the cloakroom door open, as slowly as he possibly could, while peeping through the widening gap. The double doors to the sitting-room were still open. The only light came from a single standard lamp and from the made-up fire. Over the back of the settee, two heads were silhouetted. Keith eased through the door from the cloakroom. The hall was dim but Keith sensed a movement in the further shadows. Ronnie's head was peering round the edge of the study door. Keith put his finger to his lips and then beckoned. Ronnie came tiptoeing down the hall, carrying his shoes.

As Ronnie reached Keith there was other movement beyond the settee. Mrs Muir stood up. Three men were frozen in admiration. She refilled two glasses from a carafe, stooped to put another log on the fire and returned to the settee. The vision vanished, the spell was broken.

Keith and Ronnie sidled towards the front door. One

minute later, without having made more sound than the music would cover, they were outside and the front door locked behind them. They walked softly and in silence. Ronnie was lost in reverential wonderment, but Keith was pursuing an elusive memory.

They were in the car and freewheeling before either spoke.

'You got off your mark bloody quick,' Keith said.

'Aye, I'd've been out and running except that she'd locked the back door and taken the key. Hey, d'you reckon that electrician laddie can fix her alarms for her?'

'If it goes off while he's still there, I doubt if he'll hang around. That was Denny Coutts, the boss of Coutts and Dougall. He's a lay preacher with six kids. The neighbours are in for several hours of high-speed cuckoo song.'

'Will she know she's been entered, then?'

'Depends whether she gets a local boy to shut it off or a specialist to come a long way to sort it. If she's selling the place, she may not be too fussy, I hope. What would your guess be?'

But Ronnie's mind was away on quite another tack. 'Yon was a right bonny quine,' he said. 'By God, aye! And they lace combinations she was hanging half-out-of!'

'Camiknickers,' Keith said.

'Is that what you call them then? I wonder would Maisie have anything like that. You can drop me on the corner of Upper Kirk Street if you like.'

Keith curled his lip. Maisie, who occupied a tenement flat in Upper Kirk Street, was a stout, middle-aged lady of great good nature and a ready source of comfort to several of the unattached men of the town. Her detractors said that she was ugly. Her intimates agreed, with the mental reservation that she was also free.

It is to be feared that Keith, as the father of a young daughter, was becoming inclined to priggishness. But there had been times, in his wild and itinerant youth, when he would not have turned up his nose at such as Maisie.

He drove in silence. That elusive memory was nagging at him.

In the morning, he phoned the photographer on the *Edinburgh Herald*. He wanted, he said, some photographs which would require the best of equipment. They would have to be taken with a very long focus lens, through glass. In return, he could promise a scoop when the trial came on.

EIGHT

For the next few days Keith avoided Mr Enterkin. He would have liked to discuss his fresh information with the solicitor but he was reluctant to admit how it had been obtained. He was unhappily aware that, if the police should learn from Mrs Muir that her house had been entered, he would be unable to stand up to cross-examination. Worse, he might find himself in deep trouble. Mr Enterkin was unlikely to admit that he had hinted at such a course; indeed, in retrospect Keith was not sure that he had read Mr Enterkin's words aright.

Their only contact was one telephone call, which Keith took at Briesland House between raising the dents which a careless owner had put in the stock of a Dickson Round Action.

'I've had another cable from your friend Dunbar,' Mr Enterkin said. 'Even after making reasonable assumptions in the hope of restoring the message to something resembling its original intent, it contributes little of use. This is understandable when you recall that he has no idea what you want to know; an ignorance, I may add, which he shares with myself. He suggests that direct discussion is the only suitable *modus operandi*, and mentions that he expects to finish his contract and to return home early in January. Can we leave him until then? It would give us a month in hand.'

'That's time enough,' Keith said.

'The only positive statement which I can extract from the literary garbage to which the original has been reduced is this. "Ask Calder how long he'd need between a brace of thrush." Can you make head or tail of it, Keith?'

107

'It's only what I expected,' Keith said. 'Forget it.'

'You can't fob me off like that. Expound.'

'Would it help if I explained that the farmer has a daughter by the name of Mavis?'

'Oh,' said Mr Enterkin. 'Tell me, was everybody in Newton Lauder, with the exception of myself, dividing his time between the pursuit of *Columba palumbus* and the human female?'

'It was a special day for pigeon,' Keith said.

'And, it would appear, for nooky. Was the weather especially appropriate for that also? Singularly unpropitious for outdoor fornication, I would have supposed.'

'How many sex acts would you think were going on in the world at this very moment?' Keith asked.

'I take your point. If it were not a frequent event the human race would die out. So much for that, then.'

'Irrelevant,' Keith agreed. 'How would you like to ask Mavis whether, between transports, she happened to notice anything which might interest us?'

'Under no circumstances,' Mr Enterkin said firmly.

'Me neither,' Keith said. 'Watty can find out for us when he gets back.'

Mr Enterkin, who had conducted that particular interview, had reported that neither the farmer, Andrew Dumphy, nor his wife or family had heard shots on the morning of Neill Muir's death. But Keith now had some questions of his own. He put in a concentrated burst of work to clear his workbench and drove out to the farm.

It was some years since Keith had been to the farmhouse, and at that time it had been in other occupancy. His only contact with Dumphy had been to meet him in the fields. He jolted past the now familiar area where Muir's decoys had been found, crested the slight hill and rolled down into a yard that fronted the farmhouse and was sheltered by the gable of a Dutch barn. And there he sat for a moment, glaring at a new structure which seemed to glare back at him. How in God's name, he asked himself, could Mr Enterkin have not thought to mention the existence of a pigeon-loft?

Andrew Dumphy's sturdy figure came round the corner of the barn and lifted a hand in greeting. They met beside the pigeon-loft. The wind had a bite to it and by tacit agreement they moved back into the shelter of the barn. There, blessed by the sunshine and out of that cruel wind, one could almost believe that spring might some day return.

'What kind of a year was it?' Keith asked, and listened patiently to an account, told complacently and almost with pride, of disaster and tribulation. In Keith's experience, no farmer would ever admit to a good year, but would lean against his Rolls while speaking of imminent bankruptcy.

The courtesies observed, Keith could move to the subject in his mind. 'How long have you been keeping racing pigeons?' he asked.

Dumphy broke into a cheerful grin. 'Most of my life,' he said.

'Do any good at it?'

'Aye. Had some good wins. I won more than a thousand quid on the Blue Riband race from Rennes last June.'

Keith whistled. He had known that the little birds spelt money but had had no idea that so much could be involved. 'Was that prize money?' he asked. 'Or backing your own bird? Or did you mean backing somebody else's winner?'

'None o' those. There's a pool system. My bird was placed, so I got a share of the pool.'

'That'll be a valuable bird,' Keith said.

'M'hm.'

'May I see him?'

That did it. 'Nae, you bloody canna',' Dumphy burst out. 'An' why not? Because he was shot, that's why! Sheer carelessness or ill-will it must've been. Even coming out o' the sun, you can hardly mistake a homer for a cushie. At the end of a long race, maybe, a tired bird can fly like a woodie. But this was after the racing season was over. The moult had started.' In his indignation, Dumphy had grasped Keith by the lapel and was shaking him gently to and fro. 'Not even any distance training, just what they ca' "open bowl" – just the birds being put out for a whilie each day, for exercise. An' some daft bugger goes an' takes him for feral an' shoots him!'

Keith leaned back as far as he could. Dumphy was spitting in excitement. 'What did you do about it?' Keith asked.

'Like do what? I couldn'a prove ocht. My bird might ha' been taken by a sparrowhawk or a cat. But I kenned damn fine. The bird was in the bugger's pouch or down a rabbit hole, likely. Gone, an' never came back – a blue chequer, pied, wi' a deformed left foot. I made him gi'e me my note back, an' telled the bugger never to come on my land again.'

'Who was it?'

Dumphy released his grip on Keith's lapel and stepped back. 'Nobody I'd seen before.'

'Then how come he had your written permission, for you to get it back off him? It was Neill Muir, wasn't it?'

Beneath the fury on Dumphy's face there was a hint of his earlier smile. 'I must be going daft,' he said. 'No point denying it, his wife could tell you.'

Keith felt a glow spreading through him. 'And that was the day he was killed? Or the day before?'

'No, lad, no,' Dumphy said. 'Maybe it's you that's dottled. This was last August.'

'August? It can't have been!'

'Ask his wife. She'd been with him, though she went off in that red car of hers when I started to get on to him.'

Keith was only half attending. He was trying to make sense of these new facts. 'Have you lost any other birds since then?'

'No, the Lord be thanked. The time you lose them's during the racing season, mostly.'

Keith dipped into his notebook. 'I've been on the phone to the Scottish Homing Union in Bathgate,' he said. 'About ring numbers. SU's Scottish Union. Then the year, which made it a three-year-old bird. Then SB, which is Scottish Borders. And four-two-eight-two, which is you, right?'

'Right enough,' Dumphy agreed. 'But I've lost more than one bird of that year. Has somebody found a ring wi' that on it?'

'I can't tell you that, just yet.'

Dumphy pointed a stained finger at Keith and his grin came back at last. 'Found among that bugger Muir's things I'll bet! Am I right?'

It dawned on Keith that he had been incautious. He had not yet received his prints from the photographer, because Mrs Muir had remained stubbornly at home until that very morning. 'Have patience,' he said. 'I'll tell you the whole story some time, but it's early days yet. Did you ever see Neill Muir again after your quarrel?'

Dumphy shook his head. 'Never. And it was hardly a quarrel, I wasn't sure enough. I just told him I misliked his behaviour and got my letter back off him.' Dumphy leaned closer, confidentially, and lowered his voice. 'You want a farmer who really quarrelled wi' Muir, you go and see Bob Jack at Haizert.'

'Tell me a bit more.'

'That's all you'll get from me. And don't you go saying I told you. Just mind that I didn't see Muir again after August an' didn't care if I ever saw him again.'

'How do you know Jack quarrelled with Muir?' Keith asked.

'Never you mind.'

'Do you not like Bob Jack?'

Dumphy lowered his voice further, until it was barely above a whisper. 'I liked him fine,' he said, 'until I was fool enough to marry his sister. I should've stuck to pigeons, you can aye shut them up at night. You go and see Bob Jack. But don't be thinking he killed Muir. He was here that morning about a couple of heifers. He'd been here half an hour when we walked up the hill to look at them and saw the smoke over the trees.'

Haizert Farm lay about five miles east of Newton Lauder. Keith had had occasional dealings with Bob Jack over the years, latterly on a 'cash only' footing. The farmer, whom Keith knew to be a man of uncertain temper, was also a noted non-payer of accounts rendered.

The road climbed over higher ground. It was narrow and at one point Keith had to pull into a passing-place to let an oncoming Land Rover go by. He recognized the gaunt driver as Mrs Jack. Keith drove on with rising hopes.

A new outline was beginning to firm up in his mind. A quarrel. *The* quarrel. Neill Muir lying dead. Jack deciding that the body must not be found on Haizert land. Loading Muir and all his gear into Muir's own Land Rover. Then over the hill to visit his brother-in-law, keeping him out of the way while Mrs Jack brought Muir's vehicle, set the scene amateurishly and fired the Land Rover. Picking her up on the way home.

It could fit. It could be made to fit. Whether it had happened or not, it might suffice to deflect a jury from holding the case against Jake Paterson as proved.

Where the road began to fall again, Keith pulled in. He got out with the more powerful of his two pairs of binoculars and stood with his elbows on the car's roof while he studied the ground below him. Detail was sharp and clear in the frosty air. Only one field on Haizert looked as if it might attract pigeon, an isolated field of kale, wire-fenced, and even as he watched a small flock came over the boundary from the trees on what Keith knew to be the keepered estate immediately north of Bob Jack's land and settled in the kale.

112

About half the field, segregated by an electric fence, had been cropped by cattle and a tractor was hauling more dung from the midden preparatory to a late ploughing. The pigeon seemed quite unperturbed by the machine although Keith guessed that the approach of a man with a stick would put them on the wing at twice the distance.

The car was well enough where it was. Keith stowed away his binoculars and whistled Brutus out of the back. He made sure that his gun was securely locked away before setting off across country. Twice he had to call Brutus away from the pop-eyed corpse of a rabbit, victim of myxomatosis. Keith counted the introduction of that disease among the world's evil deeds.

He timed his arrival at the kale field to coincide with the disappearance of the tractor round the corner of the byre. It had seemed from a distance that a lone ash-tree marked the only suitable site for a hide. He could now see that it stood beside a triangle of rough ground, unsuitable for ploughing, which had been used as a dumping ground for boulders and large stones. Some of these had been restacked as a rough dyke and a semi-permanent hide had been completed by lacing the fence with twigs and threading these with dried grass and weeds. There was even a four-gallon drum for a seat, with a scattering a Rottweil cartridges mingled with pigeon feathers on the ground.

The ash tree, stark in winter nudity, was ideal for a lofter. Keith looked casually around as if admiring the view and then looked up into the tree. Some shooters placed their lofters by means of poles, but many used string or fishing-line and Keith knew how easily the line could get caught up. Sure enough, there was a tangle of monofilament fishing-line, with a stone for a weight on the end, caught up around a high branch. A long tail of line hung in the still air to where the owner had managed to cut it off. Keith drew the knife from the sheath taped across the back of his belt. Although himself of only average height he could cut six inches off the end without difficulty. So the owner had not been a tall man. Keith stowed away his sample and gathered up a couple of cartridges. A small loop of string caught his eye and he added it to the collection.

The tractor was returning, snuffling along the track like a mechanical bloodhound, dragging its handler along behind. Keith walked to meet it. The farmer nodded to Keith and stopped the tractor, but he kept its engine running so that Keith had to shout to be heard. Bob Jack did not bother.

'Morning,' Keith said. 'What kind of a year has it been?'

Jack was less forthcoming than his brother-in-law. 'Nae bad,' he said. Keith had to strain to hear the words.

'Are you bothered much with the pigeon?'

'No' a lot.'

'Somebody's been doing well at them, just back there,' Keith said, persevering.

'Aye.'

'Anybody I'd know?'

'Friend of mine.'

So much for the oblique approach. 'Did you see much of Neill Muir up here?' he asked.

The farmer shook his head vehemently. 'No' for a year or more,' he said. Keith heard him without difficulty.

'Was that when you fell out?' Keith asked bluntly.

'Who says that we fell out?'

'I ken damn fine you fell out, I just couldn't mind when.'

'What's it to you?' Jack demanded.

Keith was prepared to play the game of answering question with questions indefinitely. 'Why are you so touchy about it?' he asked. 'It's not exactly unknown . . .'

'Aye, it happens. Why should I care who he carried his clypes to?'

Keith felt that he was making progress without having the least idea in what direction. He decided to back-track. 'Was

Muir up here the morning he was killed?'

Bob Jack was losing patience. 'I've tellt you, he'd not been here for almost a year.'

'He didn't come back just lately and raise the matter again?'

'At this time of year?'

Keith had thought that he was keeping a poker-face but some shadow of his bafflement must have shown because Jack laughed suddenly. 'You crafty bugger!' he said. 'You've nae idea what the hell I'm yattering on about. An' you nearly had it out of me. Well, here's what I think of you.'

The tractor went forward with a jerk, the trailer passed them and then came back, spewing the steaming dung from its tailgate as the conveyor-bed turned on its rollers. Keith jumped clear, but Brutus vanished. As the tractor drove away Keith could hear a high-pitched cackling. Bob Jack was laughing his head off.

The mound of mixed dung and straw heaved as Brutus worked his way out.

Keith would dearly have loved to run after the tractor, to haul the old sinner out of his seat and to stuff him head-first into the dung. But he curbed his anger, filing it away for future reference. The law does not look kindly on men who assault their elders, whatever the provocation; and, worse, anything to do with dung is irresistible to the media.

Brutus was unperturbed. He rather liked his new perfume. Every animal, including the human, likes to cover its personal scent from its enemies. Keith had no great objection to the familiar and healthy smell, but he knew that Molly would be more fussy. Because Brutus was in the habit of rolling in whatever he found by the wayside, some of it much less acceptable than mere dung, there was always a bottle of dog shampoo in the car. Keith bathed the reluctant dog in a burn and dried him with newspapers before allowing him into the car.

NINE

'This precognition of yours,' Mr Enterkin said unhappily, poking his copy of that document with his finger and sighing. 'I have been over it with counsel. It may take us far enough or it may not. You draw attention to certain signs and portents which, according to yourself, indicate that Mr Muir did not behave as demanded by the prosecution's theory; and then you resort to a wealth of abstruse technical detail about shooting, and pigeon-shooting in particular, to back up your arguments. Well, a jury might accept it as showing reasonable doubt, but it might not.'

Keith felt just as entitled to sigh, and did so. 'What do you want?' he asked. 'A miracle?'

'Ah. Now you're being more helpful,' Mr Enterkin said. 'Yes, a miracle would fill the bill nicely. Or, failing that, a viable alternative theory.'

'I'm doing all I can,' Keith said. 'And for all the help I get from you when I ask it, I might just as well stay at home and scratch my bum. Better, in fact.'

'That's not fair,' the solicitor protested. 'In fact, it's grossly unfair. I'm quite prepared to give of any help which is legal and practicable. But you arrived this morning with a request which was far from practicable, and I pointed out that I did not see the least hope of inducing a court of law to force a farmer, ten miles from the putative scene of the crime and who claims not to have seen the deceased for a year, to divulge the name or names of those presently permitted to shoot pigeon on his land. You'll have to give me more ammunition before I shoot at that particular target.'

'Don't bother,' Keith snorted. 'I'll hit the mark some

other way. And, if I can, I'll produce a rival theory. With luck, I may even turn up the real culprit. But you tell counsel to put me in the box and ask me my opinion of each element in the prosecution's version. I'll tear it to shreds.'

'Well, all right. But you realize that on your evidence will be staked, if not Mr Paterson's life, at least more than a decade thereof.'

'Don't remind me,' Keith said. He stamped out of the solicitor's dusty office and across the square to the shop.

That evening Keith threw a party. It was a very select party. The Calders were joined only by Janet and Wallace and by Ronnie. It was, Keith felt, an unnecessary lavishing of hospitality. But it was the only way that he could think of to bring together his selection of local knowledge at a time when they could hold a discussion not to be chaired by the now bedded Deborah.

They gathered in the dining-room at Briesland House, around the table well stocked with bottles. When Molly escaped from her maternal duties and joined them, Keith brought them up to date on his progress on Jake's case. 'Ralph Enterkin wants more,' he said. 'I think he'd like a defence by impeachment, but we don't all get what we want. Well, even if old Bob Jack had damn-all to do with Neill Muir's death, we might at least be able to use him in what Ralph calls a 'viable alternative theory'.

'So I want to know what Jack and Muir fought about. Muir can't tell me and Jack won't, Ralph can't get the law to make him tell us, and if the merry widow knows the answer she's only talking to the other side.

'I'm pinning my hopes on whoever's been shooting woodies up there. I'd guess that he's been going for some time, because he'd made his hide very comfortable, and some of the cartridges I found were almost rusted through at the base. He may know what the tiff was about. Or he may be able to give me some other bits and bobs to support whatever story I can dream up. For starters, then, does anybody know who it is that goes there? Or can you suggest anyone who might know?'

Ronnie roused himself from contemplation of an almost empty glass. 'We could ask around,' he suggested.

'I'd rather not,' Keith said. 'Word might get back. So take a look at these.' He passed round sheets of paper and pencils. 'Those are copies of a list I've been making of local pigeon-shooters. We've got to assume that he's local. If he comes up from Northumberland, we're on a loser. There's fourteen names and two descriptions.'

'The descriptions are easy,' Ronnie said. 'No bother. "Small man with droopy moustache", that'll be Willy Thyne. And "Sandy hair, thick spectacles and bad teeth", that's Joe Murchester.'

'So far so good,' Keith said. As a gesture of thanks he refilled Ronnie's glass. 'Any names to add?'

Between them, they added four names and a description – 'Tall, big ears, red nose'.

'Twenty-one men,' Keith said. He produced his sample cartridges. 'I picked these up. All Rottweil and never been reloaded. So cross off anybody we know reloads, and put a cross against anyone we can remember buying Rottweils.'

Five names came off the list and four crosses went on to it.

'Sixteen,' Ronnie said disgustedly. 'And that's not counting any we haven't thought of. You spotted that he used an auto? You can see the wee marks of the extractor hooks.'

Keith had not missed that point, but Ronnie needed encouragement. 'Well done,' said Keith. (Molly smiled secretly.) 'Put a cross against anyone who uses an auto, or a pump twelve-bore. The firing-pin's slightly off-centre, but I can't hang about until he brings it in for overhaul. And next, he uses a flapper.'

Ronnie threw down his pencil. 'How in hell could you tell that?'

Keith produced the scrap of string which he had picked up. It was tied in a loop of about eight inches circumference, and the tail had frayed and broken a few inches from the knot. He fetched his own flapper from his pigeon bag, a framework of stiff, green wire which formed a cradle for a dead bird. The loop of string proved to be the right length to go round the two lever arms which worked the wings, and the frayed end just reached to the ring on the supporting peg through which the string would be threaded.

'We'll give you that one,' Janet said. 'Who's bought that model?' And five more crosses went down.

'There was a bit of line caught up in the tree, with a stone on the end. So he uses a lofted decoy. But it was a biggish stone. He doesn't use a catapult, he throws a stone over.'

Three crosses.

'Notice,' Keith said, 'that his lofter was pulled up on a length of monofilament fishing-line. And his flapper was on braided fishing-line, although parcel string does just as well. I reckon he's a fisherman.'

'That's g-guesswork,' Wallace said. 'He could have a brother or an aunt who fishes. Or he could have b-bought the stuff to use at the pigeons.'

'It's all guesswork,' Keith said. 'Some of these guesses may let us down. There may even be two men. But it's worth a try. Who's been buying fishing-tackle?'

Janet and Wallace made eight crosses between them.

'There were matches but no cigarette stubs,' Keith said, 'and some beer can rings. A cross for a pipe-smoker and another for a beer-drinker. And, lastly, he has a dog. A large, happy dog.'

'Colour?' Ronnie asked.

'I don't know. I couldn't see any hairs. It's the wrong season for a dog to be casting. But I noticed something I've

119

seen a hundred times when I've had Brutus with me in a hide.' Under the table, the dog snuffled at his own name, and they heard his tail swish across the carpet. 'If he's enjoying himself or he's getting the scent of game, his tail sweeps from side to side, clearing away the leaf mould and dead grass until he's brushed clean a quadrant of soil. That's what I saw. And it was a big quadrant.'

'Which rules out that b-bloody great retriever of Jack Smythe's,' Wallace said. 'He had his t-tail docked after Jack backed the car over it.'

When they tallied up, every man on the list had one or two crosses. Three men tied with five. But Willy Thyne – Keith's 'Small man with droopy moustache' – had seven. 'He lives up above the canal,' Ronnie said. 'I don't know exactly where. But he drives for Barratt, the haulier.'

Primed with that information, it was easy for Keith to track Willy Thyne to his lair in a cottage where Newton Lauder dissolved into farmland by way of a fringe of sheds, greenhouses and pigeon-lofts. And there, the following evening, Keith found him washing up after a lonely supper. They had seen each other once or twice on minor shooting occasions. Thyne, although Keith remembered him as a reserved and introverted man, was quite willing to ask Keith inside and to offer him a drink of home-brewed beer.

They sat on opposite sides of a coal fire, in sagging plush armchairs greasy with age. A massive golden retriever took up more than his fair share of the frayed hearthrug. It was a bachelor scene, yet homely. Molly would have itched to change it, but Keith appreciated it as it was.

Thyne listened gravely while Keith explained. Yes, he remembered Neill Muir well. 'I been shooting cushats on Haizert for years,' he said. 'Then Mr Muir did Bob Jack a favour, got him a load of concrete pipes for drainage, and for nothing. They'd have gone on the scrap heap otherwise. Mr

Muir asked if he could shoot rabbit and pigeon on Haizert. Bob Jack was agreeable, but he asked me if I minded. I'd met Mr Muir, here and there, and he was all right. He was a big-wheel money man and I'm only a driver, but that never made a damn bit of difference to him. So I said that'd be fine.

'He had permission to shoot half a dozen other places, so I didn't see him all that often unless he asked me along with him, which he did once in a while. But when we met up we got along. Sometimes we'd take opposite ends of a field and keep 'em moving between us. We had good times. He liked to get out. Even after he married. . . . He said a man needed some time off. We got pissed together, once or twice.' Thyne heaved a sigh. 'Good times,' he repeated.

'But about a year ago he quarrelled with Bob Jack?'

Thyne stared at him. 'A year ago?'

'Wasn't it? That's what Bob Jack let out.'

'He was trying to throw you off. Six months, not a day more. Why would anyone be arguing about a thing like that in midwinter?'

'A thing like what?'

'I forgot you didn't know.' Thyne fell silent. 'Another beer?' he said at last.

Keith handed over his tankard. He could have done without another pint of the ferocious brew, but he needed to continue the mood of quiet conviviality. He patted the dog while Thyne brought fresh supplies from the scullery.

'I don't want no trouble with Bob Jack,' Thyne said suddenly. 'I value my bit of shooting on Haizert.'

'I value Jake Paterson,' Keith said.

'And you think he didn't do it?'

'Between ourselves . . .' Keith outlined his reasons for disbelieving the police view of Muir's death. To Thyne, a skilled pigeon-shooter, the arguments, which seemed only to make the lawyers' eyes glaze over, were as clear as they were to Keith. Thyne had never met Jake and yet Jake's

121

innocence became, to him, incontrovertible. Keith thought that if they could only go before a jury of pigeon-shooters, Jake would be safe. A jury of maiden ladies would probably demand the return of capital punishment. Such are the vagaries of the human mind.

'You think Bob Jack could've done it?' Thyne asked.

'I don't know,' Keith said. 'And, frankly, I don't care a lot. The prosecution has to convince a jury, beyond reasonable doubt, that Jake did it. If we can show a reasonable possibility that somebody else was guilty, then Jake's home and free.'

Thyne pondered again. 'You'll have a job with the timing,' he said.

'So will the prosecution. The police theory would require Neill Muir to have gone out at dawn and shot two dozen birds in the first hour over decoys.'

Thyne leaned forward and put more coal on the fire. 'It was this way,' he said. 'And, mind, I'm only telling you because Bob Jack doesn't know I know, and you're not to say as it was me as told you. Fair enough?'

'Fair enough,' Keith said.

'It must've been late June or early July, because I was decoying over a patch of laid barley near the west boundary. We had a nice little hide ready made, in the hedge that bounds the estate next door. I was comfortably tucked in there one Saturday morning. The birds were wanting to come in to my decoys, but they were swinging away while they were still half a field off, so I guessed that somebody was buggering about nearby where I couldn't see him and spooking them. So I waited. There was no point in moving and adding to the kerfuffle.

'Then suddenly I heard voices. I·misremember the words, but Mr Muir was asking Bob Jack what Bob was doing and Bob asked what he thought it looked like. And suddenly they was going at it like two dogs fighting over a bitch. I soon made out what it was about, 'cos Bob was trying to justify himself. He'd had enough of the rabbits breeding on Mowdiewort Estate and coming over the boundary to live off his crops, so ilka year he released a few myxied rabbits on that end of the land. They'd infect the others and that way he kept the damage down.

'Well then, I'd no wish to be a'body's body, but involved I did *not* want to be. That myxie, it's a rotten thing, just rotten. And far's I know it's agin the law to spread it on purpose. If I did get involved, I'd've had to be on Mr Muir's side, and then we'd both be looking for somewhere else to shoot.' He looked into Keith's face. 'All right, so maybe I was a feartie. What would you have done?'

'Something damn silly, most likely.' Keith pushed aside his anger for the moment. 'What about Mowdiewort? Do they know what's going on?'

'Not them, or if they do they don't care. They do no farming to speak of, just a little forestry and some game crops for the pheasants. Dare say they're just as happy to see the rabbits kept down. It's just a commercial shooting estate with letting by the day to Continental guns. And they don't do me any harm. Their pheasants come wandering on to Bob's stubbles and I can count on two brace a week during the season. I may not like it but I can see Bob's point of view.'

Keith could only see the waste of sport and meat and the cruelty of controlling a species by means of a singularly unpleasant disease. He had seen too many rabbits crouched with popping eyes, blinded by myxomatosis, waiting for death. 'There are procedures for forcing a neighbour to control vermin,' he said.

Thyne snorted. 'There are,' he said. 'But from what I hear, by the time you get any joy that way, if the vermin haven't eaten you out of house and home the lawyers have.'

TEN

There came another and more lasting thaw. Two days of rain were followed by weather so mild that, as Keith said, it would not have come amiss during the average summer. The ditches and burns ran full for a week and there was some flooding.

The thaw brought an urgent reopening of the shooting season. Suddenly the shop was busy. Keith was loaded with guns overdue for attention but which had been forgotten during the big frost and the ban on wildfowling.

The shoots also were busy. After a month spent nurturing the survival of the game birds they urgently needed to overtake their programmes, give their members some money's worth, get birds to the market in order to defray the cost of keepering and feed, and reduce in particular the number of surplus cock pheasants which would be unnecessary consumers of food in the spring. Guns like Keith and Wallace, who could make themselves available to fill vacant places on extra days, were in demand.

The thaw, and the sudden rush of activity, would seriously have hampered Keith's efforts to learn any more from the ground, had he not already exhausted almost every line of enquiry which had occurred to him.

Jake Paterson, far from being forgotten, seemed to have become the forgetter. At first peevish at his incarceration, he had been smitten by an inspiration for some further improvement to a solid-state radar system which he had once designed and which his previous employers were now selling worldwide. He was covering page after page with calculations in his precise script. His only immediate concern was for an adequate supply of pencils, paper and batteries for his calculator. His only grumble was at being separated from the computer facilities to which he was accustomed. Prisoners on remand, he found to his disgust, were not allowed access to the Police National Computer even if they had designed parts of it themselves. He also warned Mr Enterkin that his release must, repeat must, be obtained before he reached the stage for prototype work, of which he promised to give adequate warning.

Christmas came and went, and the New Year. Jake was furnished with special treats by his friends. It was reported that he had laid his presents aside, to be opened when he was less busy.

Keith had been subjected to periodic inquisitions by Mr Enterkin, so when he heard the solicitor's voice on the phone one morning early in January he expected to be summoned again to the latter's office.

Mr Enterkin, as was his occasional habit, managed to surprise him. 'I wish to come pigeon-shooting with you,' he said.

'You do?'

'Wish was perhaps the wrong word. Say rather "feel duty bound". From what you tell me, it sounds like the last resort of a mind enfeebled by either sadism or masochism, possibly both. But counsel keeps asking me technical questions concerning the matters in your precognition, questions which I am quite unable to answer.'

'You've briefed the wrong counsel,' Keith said. 'Many QCs do shoot. One of them came out to buy a pair of matched Dicksons off me last September.'

'We tried to find one with suitable experience, but without avail. Advocates cream off the fat of the legal professions,' Mr Enterkin's voice said, with just a hint of wistful resentment. 'I am told that the more expensive syndicates each contain at least one silk. Solicitors must content themselves with so-called rough shooting. That is the correct term?'

'Rough is right,' Keith said.

'Ah. And so we decided that I would be better able to fill in the details of the brief if I had seen on the ground those esoteric activities which you have been describing with the enthusiasm of Rabelais, the clarity of Schopenhauer and the credibility of Baron Munchausen.'

'You can come out with me and welcome,' Keith said, 'if only you'll promise to shut up for a bit.'

'When?'

Keith was sick of indoors. His tape player was on the blink and was too expensive to entrust to anyone but Jake for repair. The radio offered him a choice between a religious programme and German songs – *Take me to your lieder*, he thought irritably. He was doing a fiddly job for his least favourite customer, but otherwise he had overtaken his backlog. 'Like now?' he suggested.

'Today is quiet,' Mr Enterkin agreed.

'I'll pick you up in the square. Warm clothes and no bright colours.'

Mr Enterkin's enthusiasm, tepid at best, barely survived in the passenger seat of Keith's car parked up a side road south and east of Newton Lauder. From the higher ground, Keith was scanning the land south of the town through his binoculars.

'If God wanted to give the year an enema,' he muttered, 'this is when he'd stick the tube in.'

'It's a lovely day,' Mr Enterkin said.

'Too late for stubbles. The kale's about gone. We're just too early to catch them on oilseed rape, and seeding won't start until next month at the earliest. There's nothing in particular to attract them.'

126

'I thought that's what the decoys were for.'

'The birds have got to be around before you can decoy them. The few I can see are on grass. So they're taking clover, and one pasture's as good as another. There's a vestige of a flight-line down Kyneburn Strip. We'll try there.'

They drove down the hill. Mr Enterkin waited again while Keith walked across a field to confer with a man on a tractor. Then they rolled gently up a rough track and found a space to park between the track and a ditch, just clear of a gate. Keith collected a bag, a gun and the dog from the back of the car and they set off. Their route lay between a small stream and a hedgerow punctuated by occasional trees.

'I thought you chaps carried a lot more gear than this,' Mr Enterkin said.

'Some do. Jake always humps about three bags, with hide poles sticking up like antennae. Me, I like to travel light. The farmer says there are one or two cock pheasants, by the way, and he doesn't mind if we have a go. Gaudy birds with long tails. Now this,' Keith said, 'seems as good a place as any other.'

'Any particular reason?'

Keith pointed to a small group of hollies. 'We have our hide half made. Pigeon feathers suggest that somebody else has scored here within the last few days. And there are pigeon droppings around the bottom of that big fir, so that's where they like to sit and take a look around. And if I were a pigeon I'd like the place.'

Mr Enterkin looked around him. 'Why?'

'I don't know why. Just accumulated experience, I suppose.' From his bag, Keith took a length of green garden-net of very large mesh and draped it over the more obvious gaps between the hollies.

'That won't hide us, will it?'

'You are going to thread dried grass into it.'

'But I don't want to miss any of the – er – technicalities.'

Keith sighed. 'I'll do it. You can stand and admire. Or try your hand at setting out decoys on their sticks. About thirty yards out on to the grass.'

By the time Keith was satisfied with the hide he saw that Mr Enterkin had set out the dozen half-shell plastic decoys, each bobbing gently in the breeze on the rubber tip of its stick. 'Not bad,' he said. 'They're a bit tight-packed. And no bird ever stood with its arsehole up-wind, or followed directly behind another. You take the crow away out towards that thistle while I move one or two. Crows are canny beggars, so their presence reassures pigeon.'

Mr Enterkin trotted obediently out into the field and back, puffing slightly. He studied the pattern. 'It does look more natural,' he said, 'but I don't know why.'

'I'll tell you why. It's because it has the look of a real flock. How we get that difference over to a jury is for you to worry about.'

'I'm worrying,' Mr Enterkin said. 'What did you think I was doing?'

'Now the lofter,' Keith said. 'This is how I do it.' He reeled off many yards of nylon fishing-line on to the short grass, attached a lead weight to the end and with a practised flick of the catapult sent the weight over the tip of a high branch. 'Some use poles and some throw a stone over. Catapults take a certain knack if your weight isn't going to fankle itself up.' Keith attached his solid-bodied decoy to the line, pulled it up and made it fast. 'That looks pretty good. Muir's lofter looked to be too high for stone-throwing, except by a giant or a cricketer. You're sure it wasn't cricket that Mrs Muir excelled at?'

'Certain,' Mr Enterkin said. 'I follow cricket, I'd have remembered.'

'See if you can find out what was on the end for a weight.'

They joined Brutus in the hide, where he had been waiting

with the patience of long experience. Keith took two small fishing-stools from his bag and they sat down. He uncovered and loaded his gun.

'Can we talk?' Mr Enterkin asked.

'Keep it soft,' Keith murmured. 'And no sudden movements. Above all, don't look up suddenly if a bird shows up.'

'I'll try to be good,' Mr Enterkin said in a stage whisper. 'Keith, we've got a problem. Our case comes on in three weeks.'

'We've got more than a month,' Keith said. 'Surely?'

'Circumstances are unusual. The High Court has been striving to overtake the backlog of cases resulting from the strike of court officials. Now the current flu epidemic is setting back case after case – if the judge is fit, one counsel or the other is *hors de combat*. And a big fraud case was scheduled to follow us, which is now expected to last for many months. My own view is that it will go on for *ever*.'

'So they want to bring Jake's trial forward?'

'The Clerk of Session wanted to put it *back*. It's most unusual to tamper with the dates of trials once set, but you can see the dilemma, the undesirability of cutting the fraud trial in half. But the delay to our trial would have been extensive. I consulted our client. I will not repeat his exact words, but their burden was that he had been in durance vile quite long enough. He said that he would only agree to bringing it forward. And when counsels' diaries were consulted, that proved to be the only course open.'

'No chance of our judge—who is it, by the way?'

'Lord Bickenholme.'

'I've given evidence in front of him before. He's all right. No chance of him getting the flu?'

'He's just had it.'

There was a pause while a pair of pigeon passed high overhead, ignoring the decoys. 'Hell!' Keith said. 'And hell again. That doesn't leave much time. When does Watty Dunbar fly back?'

'You'll have ten days in hand.'

'Keep your voice down. After I've milked Watty of anything he knows, I may need all of ten days for more investigation. And thinking.'

'We'll have to hope not. Is pigeon-shooting always as boring as this?'

Keith kept a straight face. 'Not always,' he said. 'If I'm on my own I can sit and think, and that's much less boring. I can solve all the world's problems, sitting in a hide. And, of course, sometimes something happens.'

'You could have fooled . . . YIKE!' Mr Enterkin said as the gun went off over his head. A woodpigeon, fatally tempted away from the tree-line by the decoy pattern, paid the price, rolled over and fell, a ball of meat and feathers with trailing wings, out in the field.

Brutus was watching Keith, quivering in expectation. Keith nodded. The labrador raced out into the field, ignoring the decoys. Keith took the last equipment out of his bag and led Mr Enterkin out. Brutus was waiting among the decoys, the bird limp in his mouth.

Keith pushed a heavy wooden peg into the ground and fitted the wire frame to the top. Mr Enterkin winced as the bird's wing joints were carefully broken. Keith fitted the bird to its cradle, checked the lead of the string to the levers and tried a couple of pulls. The dead bird's wings flapped realistically. He backed, paying out string and passing it under the netting of the hide opposite Mr Enterkin's stool. 'Can you pull a string?' he asked.

Mr Enterkin lowered his plumpness carefully on to the low seat. 'We lawyers seldom do anything but pull strings,' he pointed out.

'Try it,' Keith said. 'Then, whenever I tell you, give two or three quick, firm pulls, wait a few seconds, two or three more and then stop.'

'That seems to be within my capabilities. Keith, are you going to come up with anything more by the time of the trial?'

'Keep your voice down! I don't know. Much depends on Watty. I've done almost all I can for the moment.'

'I suppose it's unfair to expect miracles of you. But even as it stands the prosecution's case might convince a jury, and they may well have evidence of which we know nothing. And we've little to counter it with except skilled cross-examination and argument.'

'And me,' Keith said.

'Just at the moment, that's not—'

'Pull!'

'What?'

'Pull the damn string.'

Mr Enterkin dutifully caused a couple of flaps. The pattern of decoys came to life. A group of pigeon, too small to be called a flock, swung towards the enticing signal. Two, less cautious than their companions, began to descend. Keith took a quick right-and-left. The birds were dead so he left them.

Keith had delayed making mention of his gleanings from the Muir home. Once the facts were out he would be committed, and who could tell where it would end? But Jake's defence might be prejudiced by the ignorance of his lawyers. Keith, himself prejudiced, believed that many defences suffered in that way. And, now that the photographer from the *Edinburgh Herald* had supplied the required photographs, Keith could point to a comparatively innocent source for his information.

'There's one important fact I've come up with since my last precognition,' he said. 'Could you find out the number of Muir's gun? Pull!'

Mr Enterkin pulled.

'He's gone on,' Keith said. 'Disbelieving bugger! Probably a policeman in some earlier incarnation. No, I wrong him. He's coming back for another look. Pull!'

The dead pigeon flapped. Keith scored with his second barrel.

'You missed,' Mr Enterkin pointed out.

'I've got four with five shots,' Keith said. 'Keep that up and I'll know that somebody up there appreciates my real value. Hang on a moment. I think I know what's been spooking them. There's a bird on its back. Also the wind's come round a bit. Shan't be a second.'

He walked out and set up his fallen birds, moving or turning a few decoys to suit the new angle of the breeze.

Mr Enterkin had followed him out. 'I could probably find out the number of Muir's gun,' he said, 'but I'd undoubtedly be asked why I wanted to know it.'

'In that case don't bother,' Keith said. 'We'll see it in court anyway. Meantime, perhaps it's better kept up our sleeves.'

'What is?'

'There's the fore-end of a gun in Muir's study. You can see it from the window, and I've got a photograph in which you can read the number.'

They reached the hide and resumed their seats – Mr Enterkin with a faint groan. 'What is a fore-end?' he asked. 'I'm becoming uncomfortably aware what the other end is. These stools are excruciating.'

Keith removed the fore-end from his gun, the tapered piece of steel and walnut which clipped beneath the chamber end of the barrels, and handed it to Mr Enterkin. 'This is the fore-end,' he said. 'I know that they found Muir's gun thrown away, barrels and stock separately. Nobody said anything about finding the fore-end. If it hasn't turned up, the police may have assumed that something so comparatively small may have been missed.'

Mr Enterkin had been looking at the gun and thinking. 'A

man could take out his gun and leave that behind, couldn't he?'

'Easily, if he were interrupted while assembling the gun after cleaning it, and then picked it up from the top and put it straight into its sleeve. I did it myself, once.'

'Well then—'

'I'll show you something.' Keith lifted the gun. 'I haven't reloaded yet. Now, I could have fired those last two shots with the gun as it is. But that's all I could do.' He opened the gun and closed it again. 'That action would normally recock the gun, because the fore-end bears on these two little cocking levers. Without the fore-end, the gun isn't recocked.'

'And can't be recocked without the fore-end?'

'Only by pushing against some fixed, flat, hard surface.'

'A fence-post, perhaps?'

'I doubt if a fence post would be hard enough.' Keith said. 'And if Muir had to hop out of his hiding-place every time he had to reload his gun, he could never have got twenty-five pigeon in a maximum of an hour and a half. And I'll swear to that any time you like.'

Mr Enterkin was looking happier. 'Now, that kind of evidence,' he said, 'is more likely to be within the comprehension of a jury.'

Without any encouragement from the flapper, a small flock dropped in among the decoys, catching Keith unprepared and with his gun dismantled. They departed again, unharmed unless by a volley of imprecations.

The solicitor paid no attention to this by-play. 'Mrs Muir came to see me about her husband's estate the other day,' he said. 'She refused to discuss the case. But, in speaking of the house, she mentioned that her burglar alarms had developed a fault. If it should turn out that you had entered the house . . .'

'Shut up and pull the string,' Keith said.

When he had eight birds down for eleven shots, Keith felt

that honour was satisfied. He offered Mr Enterkin the use of his gun, together with some terse but precise instructions. During the next hour, the solicitor wasted a dozen cartridges on the empty air but managed to collect three pigeon – two shot on the ground and one attributed by Keith to beginner's luck – and a bruised shoulder.

They were about to pack up the decoys when Keith spotted a long-tailed shape cruising along the treetops. 'Get that beggar,' he said.

Mr Enterkin swung the gun, and for once he did it right. The bird dropped in the plough behind the hedge and was retrieved by Brutus.

'I got a pheasant,' Mr Enterkin said breathlessly. 'A pheasant! Wait till I show Penny. Three pigeon and a pheasant, by God! Do you still call it beginner's luck? I just don't know what she'll say.'

Keith had a very good idea what Mrs Enterkin would say, but he held his peace.

Keith, who was usually the soundest of sleepers, lay awake that night. At first, he wrestled with a conviction that, at some time that day, he had said to Mr Enterkin some words which held the key to Jake's defence. Within an hour he had convinced himself that almost every word he had spoken had been significant. But in what way eluded him.

His last thought before sleep came was that, at some time in the past, he had encountered a large blonde who strongly resembled a younger Mrs Muir. They had met at some country fair, and she had won a prize. But for what? He tried to fit her into the contexts of dog trials, airgun marksmanship, pigeon-plucking and clay pigeon shooting, but each image was even less credible than the one before.

When he fell at last into sleep, his subconscious mind, no doubt trying to be helpful, caused him to dream that Mrs Muir, larger and blonder than ever, was propelling clay pigeons at him, and with remarkable accuracy, by means of some elastic removed from her underwear and attached to a cleft stick. If, on waking, he had remembered the dream it might have given him the connection which he needed. But then, it might not.

Keith was hardly surprised when, on the very next day, the solicitor intercepted him between his car and the shop.

'Can't stop now,' Keith said. 'Wal's waiting for me.'

Mr Enterkin ignored the ploy and detained Keith by means of a firm grasp on his tie. 'How could you?' he spluttered. 'How could you do such a thing to me? Telling me that that was a pheasant!'

Keith, using all his strength, managed to remove his tie from the other's clutch. 'I never said it was a pheasant,' he retorted. 'You said it was a pheasant, I didn't.'

'You never told me it wasn't. A magpie! Penny'll never let me live it down.'

'Never's a long time,' Keith said. 'In five years, or ten at the most, she'll have forgotten all about your old magpie. Anyway, you did a good deed. Magpies are damned awful nest robbers.'

'Well, let's see how long it takes to wipe that silly grin off your face,' Mr Enterkin said. His usually pink complexion was tinged with purple. 'I've just had a cable from your friend Dunbar. He was offered a share in some secret, and therefore probably illicit, salvage operation and is now incommunicado. He does not expect to reach Turnhouse until the Saturday evening preceding the opening of the trial.

Keith's amusement evaporated. 'Shit!' he said. 'That gives me two days to see him and then to follow up whatever he can tell me. Two days!'

'And three nights.' Mr Enterkin was cheered by the thought. 'Don't forget the nights, my boy.' He glanced around, but the square was quite deserted. 'In fact, it's not

135

quite as bad as it seems. We can give you at least one more day, almost certainly two, while the prosecution puts on its case. I can relay any technical points to you.'

'But can you get them right, I ask myself? And I was planning to be in court, to pass you notes about any technical errors in the prosecution's case or to suggest questions which ought to be asked in cross-examination.'

Mr Enterkin, now that he had vented his wrath and conscious that he might have been rash in agreeing to the advancing of the date for the trial, was inclined to be placatory. 'I dare say that I can fulfil that function, thanks to the excellent briefing you've given me.'

'You don't begin to start to commence to know the tenth part of it.'

'You have more than a fortnight to teach me the rest. Perhaps,' Mr Enterkin suggested, 'you could give me a little more instruction in the field?' The solicitor, in addition to his wish to redeem himself after the debacle of the magpie, had been much taken by the art of decoying a quarry within range.

'I've got to clear my desk and the workbench,' Keith said. 'I'll lend you a few books.'

Two mornings later, Keith was working at home. Molly was out. He was polishing high spots out of a new rifle barrel with a lead lap and jeweller's rouge – a knack which brought him a steady workload from competition marksmen – when the doorbell rang. He let it ring until his fingertips told him that the first stage was finished. Then he went down.

On the doorstep he found the rotund figure of Sergeant Ritchie, an acquaintance of long standing and very close, on one side or the other, to the boundary between acquaintance and friendship. Keith looked for Chief Inspector Munro – he did not often see Ritchie except as a shadow dogging his chief inspector. But Ritchie was alone. Keith raised his eyebrows.

In his experience, a lone policeman was as common as a single book-end.

'Aye, Keith,' Ritchie said. 'Can I come in, just a wee minute?'

'Yes, of course. Come into the study.'

If any one factor in his life reassured Keith that he had dragged himself up in the world it was having, all to himself, a study in an elegant room of Briesland House, complete with mahogany desk, comfortable chairs and shelves for his growing collection of books. It was for this reassurance that he took Ritchie into the study rather than the more sociable living-room or the informal kitchen.

Because Keith was nervous.

Ritchie did not help. He fell silent.

'Are you on duty?' Keith asked. 'Or can I offer you a drink? Or both?'

'I could do fine wi' a dram,' Ritchie said.

So far so good. Keith fetched him a dram of his second-best whisky. The best had never been subject to excise duty and so was never offered to policemen. He gave himself a stiff one, put water on the desk between then and sat down. 'Does Munro know you're here?' he asked.

The sergeant sniffed his glass, drank a mouthful and breathed out with a satisfied sigh. He made up the loss with water. 'Munro didn't tell me to come,' he said, 'and I didn't tell him I was coming. But he knows all right. He meant me to come. You ken how he is.'

Keith knew exactly how the devious Hebridean bastard was, and said so.

'You're no' fair to the man,' Ritchie said. 'He's come after you, yince or twice, when you've been a bad lad or given him reason to think it. But you ken damn fine, Keith, that he's aye been fair, and he's gone out on a limb before now if he thought justice was best served that way.'

'M'hm. Sometimes he's a good friend,' Keith said, 'and

137

sometimes not. Trouble is, I can never be sure which he is at the time.'

'Trouble is, he doesn't always know which to be. It can depend which side of the law you're on at the time, Keith. So, whiles, Munro has to play it canny until he can tell. Take the case of the mannie Muir, now.'

'Yes, I thought we might come round to that.'

'You might well. Mr Munro is . . .'

'Worried?'

'Let's say . . . concerned. See it his way. The mannie Russell, yon chief inspector from Edinburgh, he's made a good case against your friend Paterson – from what we hear, which isn't muckle. Whether the man's guilty, of course, we can't tell, but there's feelings are running too high for peace of mind. And then there's you, asking questions for the defence.'

'There's no reason why I shouldn't, is there?'

'None in the world, if all's right and proper. But is it, Keith?'

'You're asking me?'

'Aye. Of course—' There was a pause while Ritchie thoughtfully examined his empty glass. Keith took the hint and refilled them both. He made his own weaker this time. A clear head might be essential. Ritchie looked at the window through the pale amber and sighed, and sighed again. 'Mrs Muir's been having trouble with her alarms,' he said. 'The same type as your own. I thought they were supposed to be reliable, those things.'

'I haven't had any trouble,' Keith said. 'Jake does a good job when he's at liberty to do it.'

'Likely he does. Mrs Muir thought that she had a fault. She had to fetch a man all the way from East Kilbride. It turned out that she'd been using the wrong code. There was just one digit wrong. The man thought she'd misremembered the code, and so did Mr Munro at first. But she knew better. She made a right stishie and she told Chief Inspector Russell about it when he came for a further statement. They both thought the system might've been tampered with. Mr Russell's in a taking.'

'It'd take a clever man,' Keith said. 'These systems are supposed to be tamper-proof. If Russell's so sure that Muir was killed in the woods, why's he getting so uptight?'

Ritchie shook his head reproachfully while keeping a firm hold on his glass as if afraid that Keith might snatch it back. 'You're not that daft,' he said. 'If anything turns up in the house that goes against his case, he wants to show that it could have been put there.'

Keith thought that he could feel a cold sweat running down his back. He tried to look both injured and innocent under Ritchie's bland but penetrating scrutiny. 'I wouldn't do a thing like that,' he said.

'Would you do a thing like giving me your fingerprints?' Ritchie asked softly. 'Now, hold on a minute before you get up to high doh, and let me say a bittie more. When Chief Inspector Russell came to believe that Mrs Muir's alarms had been interfered with, his own team had gone back to Edinburgh. So he asked us to help. We found just the yin good print inside the control box, and it's not one of Mr Paterson nor yet of the late Mr Muir. Now, I can't force you to give me your prints, not without I arrest you first. But, if you refuse, you can see the way Russell will take it. It's maybe better you give them to me than have him come out here himself to get them.'

Keith nodded. He could see more than that. He could see the fragments of evidence which might be essential for Jake's acquittal being thrown out of court. Worse, or at least equally serious, would be his own prosecution for attempting to pervert the course of justice. He stared vacantly at a sporting print on the further wall while his mind, like a trapped mouse, raced around the possible bolt-holes only to find them blocked. The one faint chink lay in the fact that Munro and Ritchie, while not convinced of Jake's innocence, would not see a good defence thwarted out of malice. But was that chink large enough?

'Surely you already have my prints on file,' he said, probing. 'You've taken them often enough.'

'You know we're not allowed to hang on to an innocent man's prints after the need for identification is over.'

'Munro would hang on to a set of mine, rules or no rules.'

'He had a spring-clean, just the other day,' Ritchie said. 'He can't put his hand on them now.'

'That's very interesting,' Keith said.

'Of course, I could always take something with me. Surreptitiously, as it were.'

Keith got to his feet and went to his drinks cupboard, a 1920s reproduction of an early nineteenth-century *étagère*, and selected a glass. Two days earlier Molly's cousin from Arbroath, an elderly man with old-fashioned courtesy, had visited Briesland House. After accepting a dram of Keith's whisky he had insisted on washing and polishing the glass and returning it to the cupboard. The glass had been the odd one out, sole relic of an earlier set and seldom used. Keith picked it up by the rim through the clean handkerchief which Molly always placed in his breast pocket, and tipped the dregs of his own glass into it.

'You'd better take this,' he said. 'Surreptitiously, as it were.'

Ritchie took a small polythene bag from his pocket but sat looking at the glass without picking it up. Then his bland, bucolic gaze lifted and his eyes locked with Keith's. 'Afore I take this,' he said, 'just tell me, man to man and honest to God. Have you taken anything out of that house, or put anything into it?'

'No,' Keith said. 'I have not.'

'Nor tampered with anything in a way that would make or

mar evidence?'

'No,' Keith said.

Ritchie nodded slowly. He drained his own glass and pushed it across the desk. 'If you'll turn your back a minute,' he said, 'I'll just borrow that glass, surreptitiously as it were.'

ELEVEN

Keith had intended, as the date for Jake's trial approached, to spend an increasing proportion of his time on a last spurt of investigation and a methodical analysis of the alternative theories so much desired by Mr Enterkin.

But it was not to be. When Deborah contracted a mild case of the flu which was circulating at the time, Keith had managed largely to ignore the problem, leaving the extra work to a harassed Molly; but when Molly caught the bug and went to bed with a more serious attack, Keith, aided by a recovered and helpful Deborah, had to take over the household and nursing duties. Then, a week before the trial and just as Molly was getting back on her feet, Keith succumbed. The virus hit him hard. He lay in bed with a soaring temperature and a swimming head, vaguely aware that the world was rushing on and that he should be rushing along with it.

On the Saturday, three days before the trial was due to open, Mr Enterkin came to visit. He found Keith downstairs in his dressing-gown, huddled in front of a blazing log fire.

'My dear boy,' he said, 'should you be up?'

'I'm not up,' Keith said. 'And I'll not get up, if you don't mind.'

'Stay seated by all means. I'll join you if I may. Keith, you look terrible. I once had an uncle who, despite great age, only succumbed at last to the combined effects of satyriasis, dementia and alcoholism in his garden shed. When he was found three weeks later, he still looked better than you do. Take an old man's advice and go back to bed.'

Molly entered with a tray. 'That's what I keep telling

142

him,' she said. She provided Mr Enterkin with tea and biscuits, and Keith with a bowl of broth.

Keith tried the broth and made a face. 'I'll be all right,' he said. 'I'll have to be. I've got to meet Watty Dunbar off the plane tonight.'

'No you don't,' said the solicitor. 'That's one of the things I came to tell you. I've just had another cable from Mr Dunbar. He's been delayed for one more day. Some technical problem, I understand.'

'Could we get him on the phone?'

'No, of course not. He's in transit by now.'

'There!' Molly said. 'So you may as well go back to bed.'

'I've got to get used to being on my feet,' Keith said. 'I'll still have to meet Watty tomorrow.'

'I can do that,' Molly said.

'The sooner I can see him, the sooner I can start following up anything he tells me.'

'Well, that won't be tomorrow evening,' Molly said. 'You can't follow anything up late on a Sunday night. Let me fetch him. You can see him on Monday morning, and that'll be soon enough.'

'After all,' Mr Enterkin said, 'the prosecution aren't calling you, and they're bound to take two days. The earliest we could need you would be Thursday morning.'

'That's another thing,' Keith said. 'Why haven't they called me? Have they changed their theory?'

'They called your partner instead,' Mr Enterkin explained. 'It was his entry in your records.'

'I see.' Keith yawned hugely. He put his bowl down, half-empty.

'I ought to get him back to bed,' Molly said. 'What else did you want to say? I don't want to be rude, but . . .'

'That's all right, I quite understand. Now that I've seen him, I share your concern. Keith, we can expect you to be back among the living by Thursday at the latest, can't we?

143

We are rather counting on you.'

Keith stifled another yawn. 'I'll be there,' he said. 'With bells on.'

'But will you be – ah – on the ball? Well, we shall have to wait and see. Apart from telling you about the delay to Mr Dunbar, I came to give you one more fragment of information. The prosecution is still revealing the details of its case with all the generous abandon of a dog relinquishing its favourite bone, but they could hardly fail to provide us with a list of their witnesses and copies of certain statements. And even that they left until what is virtually the eleventh hour. The list includes the name of a gunsmith in Perth who, it could safely be assumed, had sold Muir his gun and would be asked to identify it. We don't have his precognition, but it transpired that your partner knew the man and had even put him under some obligation. So Mr James phoned him and obtained the answer to one of the questions with which you've been badgering me, the number of Muir's gun. I have it here.'

Mr Enterkin handed Keith a slip of paper.

'Thanks,' Keith said. 'That's good.' He put the paper, unseen, into the pocket of his dressing-gown. His eyelids were drooping.

'Go back to bed,' Mr Enterkin said.

'Take a hot bath,' Molly added. 'And don't forget your mixture.'

Keith's fever abated next morning but he slept for most of the day, awakening during the evening when Deborah, walking very carefully, brought him another bowl of Molly's broth. He squinted at the bedside clock. He seemed to be thinking through a layer of cotton wool but he could do his sums.

'Ask Mum to come up,' he said.

Molly came up immediately, looking anxious. 'Are you all

144

right?' she asked.

'No, but I'm getting nearer. Shouldn't you be away picking Watty up off the plane?'

'Mr Enterkin had another cable from Watty. There wasn't a seat for him. It'll be tomorrow now, without fail.'

'That's cutting it fine,' Keith said. 'Ask Ralph Enterkin to get a message to him if he can. He's to phone me here, any time, and reverse the charges. Can do?'

'I suppose so.'

Keith took two more mouthfuls and dozed off. He thought that he woke again immediately, but the angle of the sun told him that it was another morning already. He was deciding that he felt a little stronger and that his head was beginning to clear when he realized that the sun had gone forward again in several great leaps and Molly was dumping a tray at the bedside.

'How now?' she asked.

'Better. I don't think a breeze would knock me down now, not if I held on to something. My mind hasn't quite caught up with me yet. This is Monday?'

'Yes.'

'Jake's trial opens tomorrow?'

'Yes.'

'And Watty?'

'He got a seat on a plane but he has to break his journey in Athens. And the Greek telephone people are on strike. He'll be here late tomorrow.'

'Please God!' Keith looked at his tray and discovered that he was ravenously hungry. 'Do we have any steak in the house?'

Tuesday afternoon arrived all too soon. Keith found that it was easier to feel strong in his bed than when up and about. He tottered down to his study again and crouched over the fire, waiting for his head to stop swimming and trying to take in Molly's instructions for Deborah's well-being. An incoming phone call gave him a moment's peace.

'That was Mr Enterkin's office,' Molly said. 'Watty's plane has engine trouble. He's stuck near Paris. Mr Enterkin will be calling here on his way back from Edinburgh and we're to tell him. Watty still hopes to get here tomorrow.'

'He'd bloody better,' Keith said. 'I'm in the box the day after.'

Mr Enterkin, when he arrived, looked worried; but he refused to get excited over the delay to Watty Dunbar. 'He should be here in time,' he said, 'but even if he's not we still want you in court on Thursday morning. He got your message, but no doubt the fleshpots of Paris . . . Anyway, you may be relying too much on his contribution. What, after all, could he have seen?'

'He was overlooking the road between this house and the place where the body was found. He may be able to say that Jake didn't go by.'

'Which wouldn't help, if the deed were done the night before. No, Keith, we'll have to lean heavily on your evidence.'

'What are the chances?'

Mr Enterkin made his extraordinary thinking face. 'We don't know yet – the prosecution hasn't finished putting on its case. Sometimes,' Mr Enterkin burst out, 'I yearn for the dear old days of capital punishment.'

'You can't mean that!' Keith said.

'I do indeed. Juries used to think twice and yet again about their reasonable doubts. Now that the convicted man lives on so that any slight miscarriages of justice can be rectified, they tend to receive circumstantial evidence with less suspicion.'

Keith considered that statement and disliked it. 'What's been said so far?' he asked.

'After the opening formalities, and before the advocate-depute could get a word in for the prosecution, Richard Garrard, our senior counsel, jumped in with a complaint that the prosecution had hampered the defence by withholding information or providing it, if at all, very late. The advocate-depute said that he was sure that his learned friend was exaggerating, so Garrard backed up his complaint with chapter and verse. Then the advocate-depute changed ground and said that most of the defence's questions had been referred to the police and that he regretted if the officer-in-charge had been dilatory in dealing with them. Garrard tried to work round to a suggestion of bias on the part of the officer concerned, but Lord Bickenholme, who knew perfectly well what he was getting at, cut him off. Was Mr Garrard, he asked, requesting an adjournment?

'His lordship knew just as well as Garrard did that an adjournment would leave the accused lingering in the dungeons, almost certainly until the fraud case was disposed of—which, as I've said, looks as if it may go on for ever. So Garrard said that he was only asking his lordship to note the position, and Lord Bickenholme said that it was noted.'

'Waste of time,' Keith said.

'I'm not so sure. Bickenholme's an unusual judge. You said yourself that he's a good man. If by that you meant that he sets justice almost as high as the law, I'm inclined to agree with you. He may remember the exchange when we need him to. Anyway, the trial then got under way.'

'Did they call Russell?'

'They did not. I think they guessed that we might seek to prove bias. And, after all, he wasn't the arresting officer nor did he personally make any of the important finds. The first few witnesses were purely formal. They called the man who reported the burning Land Rover and followed him with the first police officer to reach the scene. He described the body and the vehicle, without saying anything new, and introduced all the bits and pieces which had been found lying

147

around.'

'Including the Land Rover's windscreen?'

'No. The officer spoke to the veracity of photographs of the wreckage, but none of the wreckage was produced except for electronic components and some crumpled metal fragments which I rightly suspected might turn out to be the remains of tins such as those in which explosive powders are sold. He also introduced photographs of the decoying scene. The advocate-depute asked him whether he concluded that the dead man had been shooting pigeon over decoys, and before Garrard could even object he replied that it was not for him to draw conclusions. Which rather cut the ground from under Garrard's feet when he came to cross-examine.'

'Crafty sods,' Keith said.

'Succinct. Whether accurate, time will tell. Garrard did manage to extract the information that there had been no sign of a flapper, nor of a hide. In particular, no camouflage netting.

'Next came the constable who found Muir's gun among the bushes. The barrels are conspicuously bent. Attention was called to the absence of a fore-end, but he replied that it would have been easy to miss it in the undergrowth. Do you get undergrowth beneath rhododendrons?'

'He was probably referring to the rhododendrons as being the undergrowth,' Keith said.

'Possibly. He was followed by your partner's friend, who identified the gun as having been sold by him to the dead man.

'Next came Muir's dentist who identified his own handiwork from his records.'

'Who was it?' Keith asked. 'McRobb?'

'Lumbly. I know what you're going to say,' Mr Enterkin added quickly. 'Sometimes that old soak can hardly find your mouth. I changed to McRobb myself a couple of years ago. I can only say that Lumbly came over quite

148

convincingly.

'Next, they called two forensic scientists, a pathologist and a technician. The pathologist batted first, and he was probably the least informative witness of the lot. He explained, in detail which turned several of the jury green, that the body had been in an explosion followed by a fire of great intensity and some duration, as a result of which the outer layers were incinerated and the inner parts over-cooked. The resulting tissue changes had made an analytic examination of anything but the skeleton impractical, except that, for some highly complex reason which I did not trouble to follow, he believed that death had occurred prior to the fire. He produced photographs of a depressed fracture of the skull which he believed might well have caused death, and he also stated that the damage could have been caused by a blow from the gun barrels and was consistent with the bend in the barrels. On cross-examination, he agreed that the damage to the skull could have occurred in the explosion; and that respiration would have ceased immediately, thus explaining the lack of whatever it was that he had sought in vain.

'The boffin came next, and he was still in the box when we adjourned for the night. He spoke to his examination of the Land Rover. He stated that traces of both nitrocellulose powder and gunpowder had been identified, and he made an estimate as to the amounts required to produce the effects observed. This turned out to be quite a wide bracket, certainly embracing the quantities missing from our friend's workshop. He admitted that his calculations were imprecise and commented that similar results were unlikely to occur twice.'

'That's what I said.'

'I know, dear boy, I know. The point is, can you suggest any useful questions to be asked on cross-examination?'

'No, I can't,' Keith said. 'I agree with him.'

149

'Oh dear,' Mr Enterkin said. 'Do try to make it to Parliament House in good time tomorrow. I have an unpleasant feeling that the advocate-depute intends to spring a surprise on us by way of this boffin and you might be able to suggest the right line to take.'

Keith never got to the High Court on the Wednesday. Still feeling as limp as a wet tissue and with his mind coated with treacle, he persuaded Molly to chauffeur him to Turnhouse Airport. Deborah, from being a silent child, had suddenly arrived at the stage of asking incessant and usually unanswerable questions, and had perforce come with them for lack of any friend willing to put up with her for the day. Her parents were distracted by a constant inquisition, mostly on the subject of aircraft (about which they were both totally ignorant) while they tracked Watty Dunbar's progress or lack of it by telephone. Departure from Paris, although always said to be imminent, was delayed, and when the plane at last took off and crossed the Channel it was only to experience further trouble and to make an emergency landing. at Bournemouth. Keith tried to phone but the passengers, not having cleared customs, were confined to the plane.

By this time, British Airways staff had become helpfully involved and used every means to obtain, if not accelerated progress, at least an accurate forecast of progress to be expected. When it became clear that Watty could not now reach Heathrow in time to catch the last shuttle, the Calders left, comforted with promises that Watty would be put on the first shuttle of the morning, by force if necessary.

Tired and dispirited, they arrived home to find Mr Enterkin waiting on the doorstep. The skid marks under his Rover told their own story. 'Where have you *been?*' he demanded.

Keith was in an advanced state of neurosis and ready to

bite, but Molly took command. 'We have been waiting at Turnhouse for a passenger who didn't arrive,' she said. 'It wasn't our fault, so don't go on at my husband, not if you want him to be any use to you tomorrow. Keith, go and sit in the study while I get a meal together. Mr Enterkin, would you please bring Deborah inside for me and then go and tell Keith all about the day. And,' she added, 'if Deborah asks that last question again, for God's sake don't tell her.'

Mr Enterkin, who adored Deborah, did as he was asked, which gave Keith time to wash, calm down, put a match to the logs and pour drinks.

When the two men were at ease in front of the soothing hypnosis of the flames, Mr Enterkin said more reasonably, 'Mr Dunbar didn't come, then?'

'He's in the country,' Keith said, 'and promised for the first shuttle in the morning. I should be with you for the opening of court, or by mid-morning at the latest. Will that do?'

'I suppose it'll have to. But we're running it very fine. I don't know for how long Garrard can spin out his last cross-examination. And he can't put on much defence until you're there.'

'He can call Andrew Dumphy first,' Keith said. 'He's on the list. He can say that no shots were heard that morning.'

'That takes care of about ten minutes,' the solicitor said gloomily.

'Tell Garrard to ask whether it isn't true that Dumphy's brother-in-law, Bob Jack of Haizert Farm, was there that morning and had quarrelled bitterly with Muir.'

Mr Enterkin's voice went up to a squeak. 'That'd be thrown straight out on objection. Irrelevant. Special defence and no notice given.'

'That should be good for an hour of argument if I'm not there in time,' Keith said. 'But don't panic yet. I'll be there. What's the news from court?'

151

Mr Enterkin finished his sherry and then took several deep breaths. 'Sherry seems rather tame, fraught as I am,' he said. 'Do you think I could have a stiff gin and tonic?'

'Surely,' Keith said. He struggled to his feet. His strength was returning but his knees were still like rubber.

Mr Enterkin accepted a mammoth gin and tonic and took a long pull. 'Aah!' he said with feeling.

'Better?'

'Not to say better. Less worse, perhaps. God, what a day! You were enquiring as to the *status quo*. Which, I may say, is even worse than I expected.'

'The technician was still giving evidence,' Keith prompted.

'Unfortunately, yes. And first thing in the morning he sprang his bombshell. Or whatever one does with bombshells.'

'Drop them,' Keith said.

'What? Oh, I see what you mean. Probably. Anyway, he testified that he had examined the myriad little electronic bits and pieces scattered around the Land Rover and found that they largely corresponded with the components in one of the accused's prototype radio-telephones as found in the workshop and which he produced in evidence. He stated that, with the addition of one small and very sensitive microswitch, this could be made to trigger a bomb by radio – a concept which he proceeded to demonstrate in a manner which put the fear of God into most of those present and filled the court with smoke.

'That was all very well as far as it went, and need have been no more damaging than if he had demonstrated that you and I have the necessary equipment for an act of rapine. But he then went on to testify that among the components collected by the police was a microswitch of just the type needed and which was not a part of any of the prototype radio-telephones. The accused passed me several notes suggesting questions to be put in cross-examination. These I duly passed to Garrard, who asked the questions without shaking the witness at all.'

'That doesn't sound good,' Keith said.

'That was not the end of it. A manufacturer's representative followed and testified that, although that particular microswitch is now on sale in numerous computer shops, it had only just been introduced to the market in November; and Jake Paterson's electronic emporium was one of the first customers for it. When Garrard leaned on him, which he did in cross-examination, the man admitted that as at, say, two days before the explosion that switch could probably have been bought at ten other outlets in Scotland.'

'But the damage was done?'

'It was indeed. I fear that the jury were left with an impression which may be difficult to eradicate. We only hope that you can help to offset it. Could I have another of these? It has brought new life to an ageing husk.'

'Of course.' Keith found that getting to his feet was easier this time, but his mind was still not back in gear. He topped up his own glass and mixed a fresh gin and tonic of a calibre which could only be described as lethal, while he tried and failed to think of a few words of comfort. 'What else?' he asked.

'An electrician with plans and photographs showing a cable leading from a socket in Paterson's kitchenette, out through a ventilator, down the wall, across a roof and in at the window of his workshop where it was connected to a heater within a few feet of the transmitter. He estimated that it would take less than a minute to transfer the connection from one to the other.

'Then your partner was called to prove the sale of gunpowder etcetera to the accused, which he did without giving any other change.

'Finally, Mrs Muir. She had hardly taken the stand when

the day ran out. Presumably she will speak to the last time she saw her husband, and will also complete the prosecution's case by swearing that Paterson left her abed in his flat to visit the kitchenette and provide her with a refreshing cup of tea. Thus, of course, placing him beside the end of the cable which he could have attached to his transmitter before she arrived.'

'It's solid, isn't it?' Keith said dismally. 'Nothing damning on its own, but add the pieces together . . . What do you think?'

'They may well convict,' Mr Enterkin said. 'They certainly will if we don't make a showing. Mrs Muir is the last prosecution witness. So unless you can give us some meaty material for cross-examination purposes, you'd better be there in good time. Dumphy won't be good for more than half an hour, and we'd be inviting trouble if we called Paterson before we had your evidence.'

'Did anybody look through the barrels of Muir's gun, to see whether they were clean or dirty?' Keith asked.

'Not as far as I know. The matter certainly was not raised in evidence.'

'That could be important,' Keith said. 'I've only just thought about it. Suggest to counsel that he hands me the gun and asks me whether it looks like the one which I saw in Muir's hands. That'll give me a chance to examine it. To come back to Mrs Muir, I can't think of any questions we haven't already discussed. Get Garrard to pin her down on when her husband came home and what they last said to each other.'

'Of course,' said Mr Enterkin impatiently. 'You hold the egg this way, Granny.'

'And exactly when they said it. You know,' Keith said, 'I keep getting surer and surer that I've met that woman before.'

'Don't you know?' Mr Enterkin said. The gin was getting

to him. 'I can't imagine anyone forgetting a woman like that.'

'It was a long time ago. And it's not the kind of question you can ask a lady. "Excuse me, hen, but didn't we make love in the back of my van, some time during the early seventies?" '

Mr Enterkin shuddered.

'If it's the same woman,' Keith said, 'I'll tell you one thing about her. She had a hell of a temper. She took a kick at my dog and I turfed her out of the van. And there's something else. Something important.'

'What?'

'I can't remember. But it's to do with something you've told me. You've misled me somewhere. Go over all that you've said to me about her and we'll see if we can't pinpoint it.'

Mr Enterkin stayed to supper but, in Molly's presence, discussion of Mrs Muir was inhibited.

TWELVE

As promised, Watty Dunbar arrived at Turnhouse on the first shuttle. Unfortunately, due to a lightning strike of firemen, the first shuttle left London after the court had resumed its sitting and when it arrived the time for the midday adjournment was uncomfortably close and Keith was sure that he could detect emanations of panic coming all the way from Mr Enterkin in Edinburgh. After great effort and considerable expense, Keith had managed to reach Watty on the phone at Heathrow at the very moment that the latter's plane was called. Keith remained at the phone, trying to get a soothing message to Mr Enterkin through the office of the Clerk of Justiciary.

At long last Watty Dunbar's compact frame and dark-tanned face came through the doors. They shook hands. Watty was ready for a chat, but Keith's impatience was at fever pitch. He manoeuvred them through the baggage hall at a brisk trot and whisked Watty and his bags out to the car where Molly was patiently fending off questions from Deborah.

The two men sat together in the back. 'You look pooped,' Watty said.

'He's exhausted,' Molly said over her shoulder. 'He's just had flu and he shouldn't be out of his bed yet.'

'I'll rest when all this is over. Can't waste time now. And we'll catch up with the news later.' Keith yawned. There were still cobwebs over his mind. 'Tell me everything that happened that morning, in as much detail as you remember. With necessary omissions,' he added, pointing at the back of Deborah's head.

The head switched round immediately. 'Daddy, what's a necessary omissium?'

'Ask me later, Toots. This is important.'

'Sure.' During his work among oilmen, Watty's speech had become Americanized. 'I had to be in Edinburgh by noon, about my contract, but I'd missed getting out the day before and I heard sport was good so I wasn't going to miss again. I was out there at dawn. Matter of fact, I misjudged the time and got there too early and dawn was breaking as I set my decoys. There was a flight-line developed not far away but the bug – um – beggars didn't want to know about decoys. Well, the decoys were flat on the ground and not moving, and when the sun came up they looked shiny. I wasted a few shots trying for high birds, to get one for the flapper, and when I got one I found that no way could I drive in the flapper's peg. But as the sun got higher they began to come over and I collected a few. Then, later, I had company until it was time to leave for Edinburgh. That's about it.'

'Let's start again from the beginning,' Keith said. 'You were in the corner of the wood, where the three rowans are and a blackthorn behind them?'

'That's right.'

'There's a barn on the other side of the wood, half-full of straw. That's where you met your company?'

'Where else, in that weather?'

'What time did your company arrive?'

'I wasn't thinking much about the time just then. I waited until I heard a whistle from the other side of the wood. Best guess, about nine or a little earlier.'

Deborah screwed herself round again. 'How many pigeon did you get?' she asked.

'Eleven.'

'Daddy, how many's eleven?'

'All your fingers and one more.'

Deborah looked down at her hands. 'That's a lot,' she said

157

respectfully.

Molly's mind was elsewhere. 'I bet your hands were cold,' she said.

'I was told so.'

'You keep your mind on your driving,' Keith told his wife's back. 'You're not supposed to be listening. Watty, you get a good view from where you were. Did you see smoke to the north of you, about half-way to Dumphy's farm?'

'Nothing like that.'

'Your company must have been impatient and got there before nine, then. Did you hear any shots from up that way?'

'Not a sound,' Watty said. 'And the wind was coming from that direction.'

'That's true.' Keith hesitated and then moved on. 'You could see vehicles moving on the road?' he asked. With a sense of shock he saw that they were at Corstorphine already. And he was running out of questions without having learned anything new.

'I wasn't paying much attention to the road,' Watty said. 'Traffic was going by, if you can call about three vehicles an hour traffic, but – what the hell? – who watches the cars when the birds are coming over?'

'Did you see any Land Rovers?' Keith asked desperately. 'Turn off after the zoo,' he told Molly, 'and go in where the railway line used to be.'

'I think there were one or two Land Rovers,' Watty said, 'but, again, not to notice. The only vehicle I saw to remember was a car, the ugliest bloody red I've seen in years, and I only saw that because I looked down at my decoys to see if a bird had dropped in among them, the way they sometimes do, and the white plume of exhaust caught my eye.'

Keith nodded. Mrs Muir would have been on her way to her tryst with Jake Paterson. As Mr Enterkin had implied, Eros must have been in the air above Newton Lauder that morning, among the pigeons.

'Like that?' Deborah asked. She pointed to a passing car, its exhaust steaming in the cold air.

'Just like that,' Watty said politely.

'Daddy, why do some cars make white smoke?'

'Not just now, Tootles,' Keith said absently. 'Watty, what time did the red car go by?'

'Early. I was hardly set up and hidden.'

'So the weeping widow was . . .' Keith stopped dead. There was a long pause. 'Bloody hell!' Keith said.

'Keith!' Molly said warningly. 'You won't need to talk like that when you get into the witness box.'

'I can speak "pan loaf" when the need's there.'

'Daddy, where is hell?'

'Not . . . just . . . now . . . Half-portion.' An enormous grin spread over Keith's face. His mind, suddenly, was sharp as a needle. It was all there if he could but sort it out. He scrabbled in his brief-case for paper, pencil and photographs. 'Ask your mother,' he said. 'She knows about that sort of thing. Me, I only know about heaven. Drive gently, Molly, while I'm writing. Gently but like the wind.'

Molly crossed the lights on amber from the Lawn Market into the High Street and pulled up opposite the bulk of St Giles' Cathedral. 'This child and I are going home,' she said. 'The beds aren't even made yet. Good luck. Do your best for Jake.'

'Right. We'll get home with Ralph or somebody. Leave your case in the car, Watty. Get yourself some lunch and then come to Court Three, you may be needed. Be good, you two.' Keith kissed the backs of his ladies' necks and climbed stiffly out of the car. His mind might be strong but his legs were still weak.

Behind the cathedral, Mr Enterkin was haunting Parliament Square, hopping from foot to foot.

'If you're in need of a pee,' Keith said, 'you'd better go before court resumes, you won't have time later. But before you rush off, get me in to see Jake.'

'Keith, where have you *been*?' Mr Enterkin grabbed Keith's wrist in case he should vanish again. 'We thought you'd had an accident. The prosecution's case is finished. Garrard spun out his cross-examination of Mrs Muir for as long as he could, but by the time he was getting around to asking things like her sign of the zodiac Lord Bickenholme called a halt. Garrard didn't want to call the farmer, because once he started that examination his minutes would be numbered. So he filled in the remaining hour before lunch with an interminable argument that there was no case to answer and a promise that we would prove our client's innocence. It was a brilliant performance. He never actually said anything, but it would have taken a clear and unclouded mind to observe the fact. But now we've got to make a real showing. He'll want to put you on first but frankly, Keith, if you can't come up with something more than you have already, your friend gets a free ride to Barlinnie.'

'Can I get a word in edgeways now?' Keith asked.

'Who's stopping you?'

'I think I've got all we need,' Keith said, 'if Garrard can get the evidence admitted.' He produced two pages of paper. His writing bounced but was readable. 'This is a list of things collected by the police. Any that aren't already in evidence I want brought in. The other's a list of questions for Garrard to ask me. Now, get me in to see Jake before court reconvenes.'

Mr Enterkin was studying the lists. His protuberant eyes were almost popping out. 'I don't understand all the questions,' he said.

'You don't have to. You'll understand the answers all right.'

'We've only got a few minutes.'

160

'So let's not hang about.'

Jake, in the holding cell, was brooding over the remains of an inedible lunch. He looked guilty, Keith thought, as though he had already convicted himself on the basis of the evidence.

'Cheer up,' Keith said. 'You haven't heard me telling them how innocent you are yet.'

'You look as if you'd just done ten years yourself,' Jake said gloomily. 'Can you really do me any good?'

'Have no fear, Keith is here. One quickie. Ralph's been talking about Mrs Muir as the weeping widow. I've been thinking of her as the merry widow. Which was it? What was she like when she reached your flat?'

The two constables, waiting to bring Jake back to court, were listening avidly; but it was too late to worry about that.

Jake thought back. 'Both,' he said. 'She was happy, elated. And I never knew her quite so amorous. But her eyes and nose were running. It was just the cold weather.'

'Of course it was,' Keith said triumphantly.

THIRTEEN

'. . . and tell the truth,' Keith finished. He and Lord Bickenholme lowered their hands. The judge resumed his seat but Keith remained standing. He was claustrophobically aware of the curved canopy above his head, designed to throw the witness's voice to the fifteen jurors facing him in their cramped benches.

Keith glanced around. The coat of arms high on the wall, and the cloth on the judge's bench, furnished, together with the judge's robes, the only splashes of colour in a room which could otherwise have passed for a Victorian classroom trebled in height. On his right, the judge shared his bench only with the shorthand-writer, who was so close to Keith that he could smell her perfume. On his left, in the dock which was in effect the first row of the public seats, Jake sat between the two constables. Of the three, Jake looked the least interested. The next row was given over to reporters but only two were present, one of them the youngster from the *Edinburgh Herald*. The remaining seats, which could have held 200, were about half-filled. Keith noticed Chief Inspectors Russell and Munro, seated as far from each other as possible, Mrs Muir and several of the curious from Newton Lauder.

Crammed into the space between himself and the jury was a square table heaped with a disarray of books and papers. Mr Enterkin was seated there, together with another unrobed man who Keith thought would be the Crown Office solicitor. The other five men were robed and wigged – the advocate-depute, Richard Garrard for the defence, their respective juniors and, seated with his back to the bench and apparently immobile, the judge's clerk.

Richard Garrard rose. He lifted his eyes from Keith's list of questions. He looked calm, but Keith knew that his mind must be racing ahead.

'State your name, please.'

'Keith Calder.'

'Your profession?'

'Gunsmith and shooting instructor.'

Lord Bickenholme spoke from on high. 'I have no wish to hurry you, Mr Garrard, but time will soon begin to press. Would it help if I were to mention that Mr Calder has given evidence before me on two previous occasions, once on ballistics and once on the values of guns, and that his experience and expertise are not in doubt?'

Garrard bowed slightly. 'I am obliged to Your Lordship. But on this occasion Mr Calder's evidence will concern another matter. Pigeon shooting.' He threw Keith an anxiously questioning glance and got a nod for an answer.

The advocate-depute rose. (Garrard sat down immediately.) 'My Lord, I am sure that you are as baffled as I am as to the relevancy of such evidence.'

Keith had once met Lord Bickenholme in his chambers and knew him for a kindly man and an unusually human judge; but the face between the long wig and the scarlet and gold robes looked like that of a dyspeptic frog. 'And if we do not hear it we will remain baffled,' His Lordship snapped.

Garrard was only a little less baffled than his learned friend, but he bowed again as he rose. 'Tell the court your experience of the – ah – pursuit of the woodpigeon.'

'I have shot pigeon for more than twenty years,' Keith said. 'I used to shoot for the market but now I shoot mostly for my own table. I estimate that I have shot some thirty thousand pigeon. I teach the subject on at least one course each year. I have written three booklets on the subject, more than forty articles and a book which is still a standard work

163

eight years after its publication.'

The advocate-depute seemed about to interject, but he shrugged and sat back.

Garrard glanced at Keith's notes. 'Please tell the court what you remember of the events of eleventh November last.'

'I was fetched from my home by Chief Inspector Munro of the Newton Lauder police and taken to the place where the Land Rover was still smouldering. It contained what appeared to be human remains. There were indications that the dead man might have been shooting pigeon, and I was asked whether I could make any suggestions which would help towards identifying him.'

'Were you able to give any such help?'

'I think so,' Keith said modestly. 'There was a bag of shot pigeon, containing also some spent cartridges and a catapult, lying near the Land Rover. I have asked that the pigeon be brought into court.'

The macer (the usher in a Scottish court) appeared from behind Keith and whispered with the advocate-depute, who got to his feet. 'I am advised that such a request was only received during the lunch recess,' he said. 'Several items were requested. The gun was already in evidence. The windscreen of the Land Rover has now been brought into court. The pigeon, naturally, had gone to cold store and will take longer to fetch.'

Lord Bickenholme looked at the clock and then down at Garrard. 'Perhaps your witness could move on for the moment, and return to the subject of the pigeon later?'

'Certainly, My Lord.' Garrard looked at Keith. 'Please continue.'

'In view of the facts that there was no sign of a gun and that the bag was of a type more often used to carry decoys, I suggested to the police that the man's decoys might still be in place and might give me a better indication as to his identity.

I should explain that the woodpigeon is an elusive bird and must be brought within gunshot by the use of decoys imitating a flock of feeding pigeon, and by other tricks such as a decoy pigeon sitting up in a tree.

'From near the Land Rover I could see a remarkably unmoving pigeon in a tree further north towards the farm buildings, so I went there with the police. From the car, we could see a pattern of decoys in a ploughed field. Mr Munro would not let me leave the car for a closer look. From information furnished at that time by another officer, I was able to suggest the identity of Mr Muir, although I did not know his name at the time, as the deceased. I also suggested that some of the spent cartridges might at some time have been fired from Mr Paterson's gun.'

Garrard, who had been puzzling over Keith's next scribbled question, smiled suddenly in relief. 'You say "at some time". There was no indication that the shots had been recently fired?'

'None. I was surprised at the faintness of the smell of burned powder, but at the time I put it down to the extreme cold.'

Keith stopped and looked at Garrard, who studied the list again and then lifted an album of photographs, each enclosed in a clear envelope, from the table beside him. 'I show you now the photographs taken by the police of the decoy layout. Is this how you remember the scene?'

Keith looked at the photographs and then back at counsel. 'This is roughly how I remember the scene,' he said, 'but I was only allowed to see it from a distance. These photographs show no background, and because there was no sun there is no orientation.' Keith patted the briefcase on the shelf beside him. 'I have with me some photographs, taken at my request and in my presence by a photographer from the *Edinburgh Herald* newspaper. If necessary, he could be fetched into court to introduce them, but since I only want to use them to orient the police photographs . . .'

The advocate-depute shrugged and said 'Let's get on.'

'Let us indeed,' said Lord Bickenholme. 'Produce them, subject to later objection.'

'Thank you, My Lord.' Keith produced his photographs and compared them with those in the police album. He looked up. 'By the time that I was allowed to go on the ground and to have these photographs taken,' he said, 'the police had removed the decoys. But by that time a short thaw had begun and the footprints of the officer who had uplifted the decoys were clear to be seen. From those, and from occasional signs where the decoys had protected the ground from the rain, I was able to put markers down which roughly reconstructed the pattern in which the decoys had been laid out. I introduce one particular photograph taken of that pattern and ask Your Lordship and the jury to compare it with the police photograph numbered Three. I think it will be agreed that I had arrived at a very similar pattern and that the two photographs are taken from roughly the same direction.'

Counsel for both sides pored over the photographs, which were then shown to the judge and finally passed among the jury. Keith was riding high, mentally, but his body was flagging. He took a grip on the rail in front of him.

'The jury may agree that there is a strong similarity,' Lord Bickenholme said. 'Please proceed.'

'The police photograph shows no background,' Keith said. 'The *Edinburgh Herald* photograph shows a background of the field, a strip of trees and a hill which I identify as Carlin Hill. I conclude that both photographs were taken looking towards the east.'

'A map has already been introduced which should make this clear,' Garrard put in. 'Please go on.'

'In the police photograph the decoys, which are a very usual type of half-shell decoy made in plastic, are all facing to the right of the picture, that is towards the south.'

Keith broke off. His throat had dried with the constant talk. 'May I have a glass of water?' he asked.

The macer bustled forward, but it was Garrard who handed him a glass from the counsel table. Keith sipped.

'And what significance do you read into that fact?' Garrard asked. 'I refer to the fact that the decoys were facing to the south.' He sounded almost as though he understood the question and already knew the answer.

'When I saw the decoy pattern from a distance, it didn't look natural. I felt that it had not been laid out by a skilled hand, such as that of the deceased or of the accused. Now that I see these photographs together, I'm sure of it.'

The advocate-depute was up. 'My Lord, I must object. This is the merest conclusion of the witness.'

Garrard was ready for him. 'My Lord, Mr Calder is an expert witness. He is entitled to draw conclusions.'

'With all respect to m'friend, My Lord, this is not an instance of expert evidence in a recognized field supported by professional qualifications.'

Lord Bickenholme nodded and smiled, so that for a heart-stopping moment Keith thought that his opinions were to be excluded. 'You had opportunity,' His Lordship told the advocate-depute, 'to object when Mr Calder first proved his qualifications. You will have further opportunity to question his qualifications or his conclusions when the time comes for cross-examination. Let Mr Calder proceed.'

'Please go on,' Garrard said.

'The morning was generally calm,' Keith said, 'but it will be remembered – by several other witnesses as well as myself – that around dawn there was a strong catabatic wind. That's to say a wind caused by cold and therefore heavy air from the high ground pouring down the valley through the less cold, less dense air below. That wind was from the north. It had stopped by the time I visited the site, which may be

167

the reason why the orientaion of the decoys didn't strike me at the time. Earlier, those decoys would uniformly have been facing down-wind. But anyone who has ever watched a flock of pigeon feeding will know that they will face in any direction except down-wind.' Keith, in full flood, let his enthusiasm carry him away. 'They don't like the cold wind up their bums. I beg your pardon, My Lord,' he added. 'I forgot where I was.'

There was a moment of shock. Then one of the jurors gave a snort of laughter. An amused murmur ran round the spectators and was quickly silenced.

'Well, don't forget again,' Lord Bickenholme said. There was amusement in his voice.

'That's only what I say to pupils,' Keith said apologetically. 'The real reason is the lay of the feathers. The experienced shot sets his decoys facing predominantly up-wind. And there were other indications. The ploughed field was not a place where pigeon would feed. And at that time of year, with the ground comparatively bare, a hide would have been essential; and I could find no trace of a hide having been made or used.'

Garrard read out the next question. 'What do you conclude from these observations?'

'I concluded that the scene had been set by somebody who had watched an expert shooting over decoys without understanding the principles. At first, I thought that Mr Muir must have been killed elsewhere that morning, and that the whole scene had been moved in case the real site might point to the murderer. I now believe that the true explanation requires a more radical look at the facts.'

Richard Garrard came to the last question. 'Do you,' he read, 'have a rival theory which explains all the facts in evidence? From—' He bit off the words. Keith's last note read *From here on, play it off the cuff.*

'All the facts in evidence,' Keith said, 'and some which

168

have not yet been brought out.'

The atmosphere had become charged. Whispers, the rustle of sweet-papers and the turning of pages had ceased. Keith, with all attention and responsibility weighing on him, was about to succumb to an attack of stage-fright. The tension broke when, after a slight disturbance behind Keith's back, the macer tiptoed forward and stooped to whisper – Keith could not be sure whether it was to the Crown Office solicitor or to the advocate-depute. The latter got to his feet. Keith thought that an advocate's career might well be curtailed by arthritis in his knees. Up and down, up and down . . .

'My Lord, the pigeon have now been brought into court. I dispute their relevance, but they are available.'

Garrard met Keith's eye and read the signal. 'I would like Mr Calder to have the chance to examine them now.'

After discussion, the dead birds were laid out along the shelf which fronted the jury box. Keith had time to gather his thoughts and to remind himself not to let his courtroom manner slip again.

When all was ready, the court again fell silent. Keith stepped down and walked across. Of the five jurors in the front row, four were frankly curious while one elderly lady of spinsterish appearance had turned her face away.

Keith laid one finger on the neck of the first pigeon and turned away. 'Thank you,' he said. 'That's all I wanted. I'm now quite certain.'

The advocate-depute rose yet again. 'My Lord, I protest. This must be the merest histrionics, verging on necromancy. What could the witness possibly have learned from such a gesture?'

'No doubt the witness is about to inform you,' Lord Bickenholme said patiently.

'I shall be happy to,' Keith said. 'If counsel would join me, I'll ask the advocate-depute to repeat my examination and to tell Your Lordship and the jury what he finds. That might save passing dead birds from hand to hand and getting feathers over everybody.'

'I am agreeable,' Lord Bickenholme said, 'If the advocate-depute is equally so.'

Both senior counsel came to the jury box. 'Put your finger here,' Keith said, 'on that bulge in the neck. Prod it and tell me what you can feel.'

Tentatively, the advocate-depute fondled the neck of one of the pigeon. Garrard did the same with another bird.

'Gravel?' the advocate-depute suggested.

'Grain,' Keith said. 'It feels very like gravel. Perhaps the advocate-depute would like to borrow my penknife and open one of the birds' crops?'

'I'll reserve that privilege for Mr Calder on cross-examination. Are we finished here?'

'I would like to draw the court's attention,' Keith said, 'to the fact that one bird is a noticeably different colour from the others and has a deformed left foot. It is, in fact, a racing pigeon. I would also like to call your attention to the fact that this bird,' he lifted the stiff corpse of a large woodpigeon, 'has evidently had both upper wing-joints broken. May I suggest,' he added, 'that the birds go back to cold storage until they are needed again? They go off rather quickly in a warm room.'

Keith returned to the witness-box. The pigeon were removed.

'You were about to explain your theory as to Mr Muir's death,' Garrard said.

'Before I do that,' Keith said, 'I'd like to make a couple more points – now that I've seen the pigeon. One of the most useful tricks in decoying is to put a dead bird into a frame which will cause the wings to flap when a string is pulled. This adds life to the decoy pattern and catches the eye of birds still a long way off. Because birds stiffen quickly after

170

being shot, it's necessary to break the upper wing-joints. That bird with the broken wings had been used in a flapper. But on the morning when Mr Muir died the ground was frozen too hard for the necessary peg to be drive in. Only one of those of us who were out that morning managed to make use of a flapper.

'My other point is the racing pigeon. Andrew Dumphy, the farmer, has been called to give evidence for the defence. I am positive that he will identify the racing pigeon as one which disappeared, believed shot, last August.'

The advocate-depute rose again to his feet. 'My Lord, I object strongly to this manner of presenting the case for the defence. This witness is putting statements into the mouth of other witnesses. The court is entitled to a clear statement by my friend, setting out what he expects to prove, and then to hear the witnesses called in proper sequence.'

The advocate-depute bobbed down and Garrard bobbed up. They reminded Keith of a pair of hens, pecking in turn at the feed bowl.

'In normal circumstances,' Garrard said, 'my friend would be entitled to his objection. But, My Lord, the circumstances are exceptional. This witness was asked to carry out an investigation on behalf of the defence. In this, he was hampered by the reluctance of the prosecution to release any information regarding the details of the case which we were to answer, or to give sight of physical evidence which is only now being produced. It also happens that during the last few weeks Mr Calder was unavailable due to the influenza virus now epidemic. And, finally, information was obtained only this morning from a man newly returned from abroad who will be called later to give evidence.

'Your Lordship will appreciate that, in the circumstances, my brief is somewhat out of date. If time permitted I would ask for an adjournment in order to take fresh precognitions, cite further witnesses, make a fresh opening statement and

171

proceed from there. But, with all respect M'Lord, time does not permit. In the event of an adjournment, Your Lordship might find it difficult to appoint a date on which to resume which is not unacceptably remote.

'There is, however, a simple solution. If Your Lordship will accept that much of what remains to be said by this witness is in the nature of a preliminary statement being made on my behalf, and that any statements made in that capacity will be properly testified in due time, we can identify separately as we go along any matters to which the witness is speaking out of his own knowledge and which will therefore be subject to cross-examination.'

Garrard and the advocate-depute did their seesaw act.

'My Lord, such a procedure can lead only to confusion.'

Lord Bickenholme looked at Keith. 'You are only just recovering from flu?'

'Yes, My Lord.'

'Would you care to give the rest of your evidence seated?'

'Thank you.' Keith began to sit down.

'Don't try to balance yourself on the miserable little shelf,' Lord Bickenholme said. 'I have observed for years that it is extremely uncomfortable. Fetch Mr Calder a chair. We will then proceed as suggested by Mr Garrard. I feel sure that Mr Calder can avoid confusing the two parts of his testimony, and I am confident that I can guide the jury in order to avoid confusion in their minds. If the advocate-depute is confused he can blame his own tactics. The necessity might not have arisen if the defence had been allowed to prepare their case at the proper time. Let the witness proceed.'

The advocate-depute sagged into his chair and began a muttered argument with the Crown Office solicitor.

'This is how I see it,' Keith said. He pitched his voice up and spoke more slowly for the benefit of the shorthand-writer, who was now almost out of sight from his new position. 'Take the following facts. Decoys badly laid out, facing down-wind, placed where there had been no feeding for pigeon since the grain stubbles were ploughed on a date to which the farmer can speak. The absence of a hide. The presence of shot pigeon which appear to have been feeding on stubbles, at a time when pigeon were feeding on kale or clover. And a racing pigeon which the farmer will testify disappeared, believed by him to have been shot by the late Mr Muir, on an occasion last August.

'I can conceive of only one possible explanation, and that explanation is supported by other evidence. I suggest that the defence later calls the photographer for the *Edinburgh Herald* whose photograph of the decoy site you have already seen. On my instructions he took further photographs through a window of the Muir house which prove conclusively that Mr Muir never left his home that morning intending to shoot pigeon.

'I believe that Mr Muir was killed in August or early September, at some time after an occasion which Andrew Dumphy, the farmer, will describe, on which Mr Muir shot a number of pigeon on his land and was accused by the farmer of having shot a valuable racing pigeon. Mr Muir denied it, but that may have been the kind of cowardly reaction to which we are all subject at times. I believe that Mr Muir put all his pigeon into the freezer, still in the feather.

'I believe that he may well have been killed, as has been suggested, by a blow from his own gun-barrels. If, as I suppose, this happened while his gun was dismantled for cleaning after that or some other shooting trip, it would explain why his complete gun was not found but only two components of it. The other is still at his home.

'I further believe that his body was then placed in a deep-freeze and kept there until shortly before it was found in the burning Land Rover.'

A buzz of comment was cut short. In dead silence except for the clicking of her heels, Mrs Muir walked out of the courtroom. Eyes followed her. So also, Keith noticed, did Chief Inspector Munro.

'It is evident, My Lord,' the advocate-depute said, 'that Mr Calder's theory would aim to incriminate a specific individual. As such, it would be a special defence by impeachment, for which notice should have been given.'

Garrard, who had sat down, stood again. He was a stout man, and Keith thought that the exercise was probably doing him good. 'It is also evident,' he said, 'that Mr Calder has been trying very hard to avoid naming names.'

'And,' said His Lordship, 'has been considerably hampered thereby.' He looked up for a few seconds at the Greek key pattern around the cornice before going on. 'During preliminary debate, the advocate-depute argued that he had given advance information to the defence and implied that the length of the period in advance was only relative if not irrelevant. I take the view that so short a period would have made it extremely difficult for the defence counsel to consider the prosecution's case, obtain adequate precognitions from the prosecution's witnesses and consult Mr Calder afresh. We have already been told that this is at least partly the reason why the defence's rival theory is only now being put forward.

'There is a saying, no doubt as familiar to the present witness as to anyone, about sauce for the goose. Furthermore, if we fail to conclude this trial expeditiously a man as yet unconvicted may have to wait in prison for some considerable time before the trial can be resumed.

'I therefore propose to get all the evidence in, and in the presence of the jury, even if this court has to sit through the weekend to do it. It may be that Mr Calder's theory may be untenable and can be discounted.'

'Very probably, My Lord,' said the advocate-depute.

'On the other hand, it may be that Mr Calder's theory

174

proves so convincing that the advocate-depute will concede the case. In either of those eventualities, no harm will have been done. If, however, the new defence falls between those two poles I will, very reluctantly, grant an adjournment so that the prosecution can investigate the fresh evidence. Mr Calder, please complete your exposition and we can then proceed towards hearing other witnesses in support of it.'

'Thank you, My Lord. I may name names?'

'You may.'

Keith was very tired. He sipped more water and struggled on. 'Andrew Dumphy, the farmer, will tell the court that on that day last August when he accused the late Mr Muir of shooting his racing pigeon, Mrs Muir had also been present as a spectator, and that she had left early. She was in her own car because she disliked sitting in her husband's Land Rover. I shall come back to this point.

'The fatal quarrel may even have occurred that same day. As to the reason for such a quarrel, I believe that it is not essential even for the prosecution to prove motive and that it would certainly not be necessary for the defence to do so. But it seems to have been common knowledge, and therefore should not be hard to prove, that Mrs Muir wished her husband to give up the rural life when he retired. Their trip together to Mr Dumphy's farm may have been an effort on his part to interest her in country activities. I am advised that Mr Muir had decided to remain where he was and to invest his retirement sum in partnership with the defendant. That, I think, is already in evidence.'

'It is,' said Garrard.

'That may have been enough to provoke a disagreement. Witnesses may be found to confirm that Mrs Muir is a woman given to sudden loss of temper. She snatched up the barrels of the gun which her husband was cleaning and clouted – er – struck him with them, fatally.

'When she had calmed down, she realized that she had

175

more than one problem to face. She didn't want to be prosecuted, of course. Additionally, her husband had not been a rich man. He had only been with his last employers for a short time, so it's to be supposed that her entitlement to a widow's pension would not be large. But he had been persuaded to take an early retirement in return for a lump sum in compensation. He was already on his retirement leave at the time of his death. Whether or not his compensation depended on his living past his actual retirement date doesn't matter, it's enough that Mrs Muir may have thought that it did. Mr Muir's solicitor—' Keith caught Mr Enterkin's eye '—can speak to the financial details.

'Mrs Muir decided to postpone the day of her widowhood. She is of an athletic build and her husband was a small man. She deposited him in his own deep-freeze alongside his pigeon and gave out the story that he was spending his retirement leave on a tour of those sporting hotels which arrange shooting for their guests. There are a whole lot of such hotels. I have telephoned to more than thirty of the most likely without finding a single one which he visited last autumn, although several knew him from earlier visits.

'She now required a manner of death for her husband which would make it difficult or impossible for pathological examination to detect that the body had ever been frozen. Virtual cremation in a burning vehicle would have been the most practical.

'She did not feel confident of faking an accident so she decided to set a scene in which, if murder was detected, she would not be suspect. And she also decided to provide herself with an alibi. She needed, in fact, a lover. It may have been coincidence that the man she took up with was the accused, Jake Paterson, who was also the man who had been her husband's choice for a future partner. She may or may not have intended to incriminate him. Personally, I think not.

176

But she must have seen the advantages of having access to his stock of explosives. She also took some used cartridges, in order to make up the number she needed. Her husband had been a tidy man who collected and disposed of his spent cases, and if the pigeon in her freezer were the product of more than one of his outings she would have found herself with more dead birds than used cartridges. Foolishly and out of her ignorance, she decided to make up the number of cartridges rather than discard some of the birds.

'At the convenient time, once her husband's retirement date was past, she prepared to act. She made an early morning appointment with her lover.

'At some stage, she threw away the stock and barrels of her husband's gun, but she did not know enough to take the fore-end, which I saw still in her house, and had photographed, after the event.

'Overnight, she must have been hard at work. She must have made two journeys and walked home, or at least made her way home, between them. She had to bring the Land Rover, with her husband's body, to where it later burned. And she had to bring her own car to the same place. Then she had to place the decoys, and for that she must have waited until shortly before dawn, because the moon did not rise until five am that day.'

Keith paused and took another sip of water. The public seats had filled up during the afternoon, but he was speaking into a deathly hush.

'When I first visited the site, I noticed that the decoy in the tree had been pulled up on a light line passing over a high branch. The usual technique for doing that is to use a boy's catapult. I do it that way myself. There was such a catapult with the bag of pigeon. You need to be good with the catapult and lob your weight cleanly over a single branch or you get the line fankled up among all the twigs. That had me thinking of this as a man's crime. And the solicitor for the defence put me further off the track when he agreed that Mrs Muir was an athletic lady and had been a successful sporting competitor but he referred to "squash or badminton or something". I think that those were his words. Eventually, I remembered having seen her before. It was at a country fair. She had been a successful competitor at the archery, and had then visited the catapult stand and walked off with most of the prizes.'

'Could the witness speak up please?' the shorthand-writer asked.

Keith spoke up. 'Lastly, she would have wanted to be well on her way to her alibi before the Land Rover blew up. Sophisticated timers would have been beyond her skill, and traces might have been found. I would suppose that a long candle in a shallow tin of gunpowder would be nearer her mark. She would have found by experiment that the candle would sometimes extinguish itself in molten wax. It would be surer if a hole were drilled through the base of the candle and filled with gunpowder. I think that I saw, through Mr Muir's study window, scorch-marks on his workbench which might have resulted from such experiment. If I am right, there would also be traces of candle wax. Investigation by the police would certainly determine whether or not such signs were there.

'That, My Lord, concludes my theorizing, but I would like to bring to your attention some supporting evidence. First, may I see Mr Muir's gun?' The gun was fetched by the macer from the table behind Keith. The bend in the barrels was conspicuous and, to Keith, offensive. He looked first at the number on the tang of the trigger-guard. 'The number on this gun agrees with the number on the fore-end in the photographs which will be produced. Also, the insides of these barrels are clean. The gun has not been fired since it was cleaned. I find it extraordinary that the officer in charge of this investigation either missed or suppressed that fact.'

'Please refrain from criticizing the police,' Lord Bickenholme said. But he spoke gently. 'Continue with your evidence.'

The gun was passed round the jury. Several men tried to look through the barrels.

'Next,' Keith said, 'I will call your attention to the windscreen of the Land Rover. When I saw the scene, I noticed that the windscreen had blown out in one piece and had landed unbroken in a bush. I noticed that it was scratched. May I see it please?' The macer brought the windscreen and, on Keith's instructions, turned it round. Keith nodded. 'Please show it to His Lordship and to the jury. They'll see the scratches. And they'll see that they are circular or spiral. Look against the light. Scratches just like that are only too familiar to those of us who let our wives drive our cars. They get made by a lady who wears jewelled rings and uses the back of her hand to wipe the mist off a windscreen. Mr Dumphy and others will state that Mrs Muir never sat in, let alone drove, her husband's Land Rover. And a mechanic from Ledbetter's Garage in Newton Lauder can testify to putting a new windscreen in Mr Muir's Land Rover shortly before Mr Muir's death.

'Finally, I suggest that the defence calls Mr Dunbar, the witness who arrived back from the Middle East only this morning. He informed me, and will inform the court, that he was also out after pigeon that morning. His position overlooked the road, perhaps half a mile south of where the Land Rover was found. He saw a car go by which may be assumed to be Mrs Muir's, on her way to her tryst with the accused. Mr Dunbar decribed the colour of her car, and if there is another like it around Newton Lauder I've never seen it. His attention was drawn to the car by "the white plume of the exhaust" as he put it. It is common experience, My Lord, that in cold weather a car's exhaust will produce visible steam while it is cold but not after the engine and

179

exhaust have heated up. I suggest that, if Mrs Muir had done the five or so miles from her home non-stop, the exhaust of her car would not still have been visible.

'That is all. I have no more observations to offer.'

'I have no further questions for this witness,' Garrard said, his tongue firmly in his cheek.

Lord Bickenholme looked at the courtroom clock. 'We have already passed the hour for adjournment,' he said, 'and no doubt the counsel for both sides would like time for thought before we proceed. We will adjourn until ten am tomorrow. The police will visit the house of the late Mr Muir and investigate as suggested by Mr Calder. Mr Calder, you will attend in the morning for cross-examination. In the meantime, you must not discuss your evidence with anyone at all.'

There was whispering between Mr Enterkin and Garrard, who rose for the last time. His face was lit with mischief. 'It is for the jury to return a verdict, My Lord,' he said. 'But it must already be evident that the defence has provided an explanation of the facts at least as credible as that of the prosecution.'

'If you are about to ask me to dismiss the case, you are somewhat previous.'

'I was about to suggest, My Lord, that bail in a murder case is unusual but not unprecedented. My client is a man of substance. He will not disappear before the verdict.'

'But Mr Calder may well not stand up to cross-examination—'

'He may well not,' The advocate-depute said, without rising.

Lord Bickenholme frowned. 'Your client,' he said to Garrard, 'can spend one more night in detention—' there was a long pause '—before hearing the jury's verdict.'

'And,' Mr Enterkin said as he drove slowly past the last lights of Gilmerton and out into the dark countryside, 'if that wasn't a strong hint then I don't know one when it jumps up and down in front of me.'

'Can't comment,' Keith said, yawning. 'Not allowed to discuss the case.'

'Who's talking to you? I was addressing your friend in the back seat. We can't prevent you listening, of course.'

'Who's listening?' Keith said. The taste of exhaustion was in his mouth. Virtue had gone out of him.

'I certainly took it for a hint,' Watty Dunbar said from the back seat. 'Surely it's all over bar the shouting? The prosecution can hardly make out that theirs is the only reasonable explanation.'

'You may be right,' Mr Enterkin said. 'Quite possibly. If Keith stands up to what's certain to be a pretty searching cross-examination. And, of course, always providing that you and the other witnesses – not excluding my own self – do their stuff. It really is a pity that he can't discuss the case. I'd have liked to tell him he was quite right about the archery. I remember now. Some of the trophies on the Muir mantelpiece feature minute figures of toxophilites in Cupid-like attitudes. And I would also have liked to give him some advice regarding cross-examination.'

'Give it to me,' Watty said. 'Keith's been there before.'

'So he has. Bear in mind,' Mr Enterkin said, 'that opposing counsel only wants the truth. He is not your enemy – or, if he is, then it is for the counsel who called you to jump to your defence. Tell the truth. If you're sure you're right, stick to your guns; but don't be afraid to admit it if he's shown you that you've made a mistake. If the going gets rough and you are being savaged, it sometimes helps to picture the other man sitting on a chamber-pot, or in some other equally ridiculous situation. . . .'

Keith missed the rest of Mr Enterkin's valuable advice. Exhaustion took over. The solicitor's voice became hollow and distant, and Keith dozed off. He awoke, still groggy, as

Mr Enterkin pulled up at the door of Briesland House. He sat up and rubbed his face.

'I'll pick you up in the morning,' Watty said. 'Mr Enterkin has to go back at some unChristly hour for a lawyers' confab. And my car'll need exercise after being idle since November.'

'That seems sensible,' Mr Enterkin said. 'Now we'll just come in for Mr Dunbar's cases.'

Molly met them in the hall. 'How did it go?' she asked.

'You should have stayed,' Keith said. 'I was magnificent.'

'I bet.' She looked at Mr Enterkin.

'He was, as a matter of fact,' Mr Enterkin said. 'But he can't discuss it.'

'A quick dram,' Keith said. 'Something to eat. And then sleep. Good night, you two.'

He tried to follow that sensible programme, but sleep was slow to come. Through his mind ran a number of questions which he would prefer not to be asked on cross-examination.

FOURTEEN

Keith never had to face the ordeal by cross-examination. He was hurrying to finish his breakfast at eight the next morning when visitors arrived. Mr Enterkin and Chief Inspector Munro arrived together. They seemed to be on better terms than usual.

Keith joined them in the hall. 'This had better be quick,' he said. 'I can't hang about. And if you're driving yourself, Ralph, you're going to be late. At the speed you drive, you won't be there before they break for lunch.'

'None of us need hurry,' Mr Enterkin said. 'It's virtually over.'

'Then come into the dining-room,' Keith said. 'I can finish my toast and you can share the coffee. Do I need to phone Watty?'

'He knows.'

Keith fetched more cups and emptied the percolator into the coffee pot. They sat down at Molly's polished table. It occurred to Keith that Munro was looking tired and hungry. 'Molly always makes far too much toast,' he said. 'Would you like to help me finish it?'

'That would be kind,' Munro said. 'I have been up all night, and with no time for eating. I will use your plate.'

'Penny gave me a cooked breakfast an hour ago,' Mr Enterkin said comfortably.

Keith spread himself one final piece of toast. He took it in his fingers and passed his plate to the chief inspector. 'I saw you follow Mrs Muir out of the courtroom,' he said.

Munro nodded. 'It was already obvious, the direction your evidence was taking.'

'You thought that she might skip out?'

But Chief Inspector Munro had already filled his mouth. His long and usually moody face bore an expression of sublime pleasure. '*Taitneach*! Delicious!' he said at last. The Hebridean lilt in his voice was so strong that Keith half expected him to break into song. 'I did not realize how hungry I was.'

'We can wait.'

'Just let me eat this and wash, and I shall be ready to talk.'

A few minutes later Munro, with six pieces of toast and much coffee inside him and his face freshly scrubbed, was as good as his word. 'No,' he said, 'I did not expect her to skip out. I thought that she might burn the house down. You had reached the point of telling the court that there was evidence in the house, but you had not said what it was. And I knew that the buyer she thought she had for the house had not been able to get his mortgage; because he was one of my men. It might have suited her fine to destroy the evidence and to gain the insurance money, all for the price of a match.

'I followed her, and she went straight to the Grassmarket where her car was parked, and I caught up with her just as she was getting into it.'

'What did you do,' Keith asked. 'Make her produce her driver's licence?'

'I did exactly that, while I thought about it. I wanted to keep her away from her house until it had been searched properly and in my presence. So I asked her to hurry home so that she could let our men in.'

'You crafty old devil,' Keith said.

'Thank you. One thing I have learned about you Lowlanders is that if you want them to do one thing you must ask them to do another. She told me to go to hell and walked off. I thought of following her but decided, wrongly perhaps, that that would do no good. Instead, I found a telephone and called my office. I told the duty officer to get a car out to the house. Under no circumstances was Mrs Muir, or anybody else, to enter that house until it had been searched in my presence.

'I came back to Parliament House just in time to hear the last of your evidence and the Judge's directions. I waited to get hold of Chief Inspector Russell, who went straight away to get a search warrant. When I got to him, he was on the point of leaving for Newton Lauder. By that time I was becoming anxious about the woman. I knew that I should not have let her away on her own. So I told Russell that he would not be wise to leave before seeing whether she was at her Edinburgh flat, because if she was not at Newton Lauder and he had made no attempt to contact her then he would be out of order to break in. He did not like it, but I told him of a similar case in which an officer was ordered to pay for a new door out of his own pocket.'

'Was that true?' Mr Enterkin asked quickly.

'We will not go into that. It took us some time to find out the address of the flat, the purchase being so recent, and when we arrived at last we could get no answer. Russell was for leaving immediately for Newton Lauder, but by that time I was seriously worried. A neighbour said that Mrs Muir had arrived some time ago and had not left again. So I went to the janitor for a master-key and we went inside.'

Munro paused to refill his cup. Keith waited, his scalp prickling.

'It is a nice flat,' Munro said, 'and she had decorated it well although not to my taste. Many of her personal things were there already; she was prepared to move at once if she sold the house.

'It was clear that she had gone there straight from the Grassmarket. She had spent a little time dusting and polishing and she had lit a fire. There is great comfort in a fire. She had sat down with a large brandy, and had used it to help her down with a whole lot of sleeping tablets. She was breathing when we got to her but she died on the way to hospital.

'There was a letter beside her. In it, she admitted everything.'

In the silence which followed, Keith tried to hold his mind back from the thought that a woman, one of the many who had loved him in the back of his van in the wild old days, had gone through a cleansing ritual, in the longed-for home which she knew she would never occupy, and had then taken her own life because of his interference. He preferred to remember that because of that interference Jake would walk free.

'What happens now?' he asked.

Munro choked off a yawn. 'Forgive me,' he said. 'I must away to my bed soon. I am getting too old for these all-night affairs. Mrs Muir's letter bore out your reasoning in a way that was hardly canny. We managed to find the Crown Office solicitor, and he caught the advocate-depute on his way to a dinner. I doubt that he got to his dinner before the pudding, poor man. There will have to be an investigation, of course, but the upshot was that the advocate-depute will go into court this morning and put the letter into evidence. He will then move for an adjournment and will not oppose the granting of bail. Your friend will be free in an hour or two. Mr Enterkin has ordered a car, to fetch him home.'

'So it really is all over,' Keith said.

'Not quite,' Mr Enterkin said. 'There is one piece of evidence, Chief Inspector, which Keith's theory doesn't explain.'

'That is true,' said Munro. 'But there are always loose ends.'

'At the very beginning of this case, you took the trouble to warn Keith that Chief Inspector Russell would not be unbiased. That seemed extraordinary. After all, an innocent man should not fear even a biased investigation. Just now

186

you said, twice, that the Muir house was to be searched *in your presence*. After you had taken that decision, you seem to have stuck to Chief Inspector Russell as if to the proverbial blanket.'

Munro looked out of the window and said nothing. His long face, tired as it was, seemed to have been drained of expression by some effort of will.

'There are some police officers,' Mr Enterkin said, 'who, when they believe their prisoner to be guilty but their case is incomplete, are not above fabricating such pieces as are missing. Was it in your mind that Russell is one of them?'

'I never said so,' Munro said. He was speaking with great care, in the pedantic style of the Gaelic-speaker afraid of tripping over the English language. 'That is not a trait of which I would lightly accuse a brother officer. I will only say that Mr Russell is known to hold a grudge. And he is now a very angry man. It could be said that he wants blood. Mr Paterson, whom he looked on as his persecutor, seems to be slipping out of his grasp – thanks solely to you, Mr Calder. On whom do you suppose his rage is turning?'

'Can't think,' Keith said huskily.

'You mean that you prefer not to think. But it would be better if you gave these things some thought. For my own reasons, about which you may think what you like, I stayed with Russell while a search was made, first of the flat and then of the house. We have not long finished. In the flat, I will only mention a large, chest freezer, and there was an empty space in the larder of the house where it seems to have stood. The marks of the feet correspond. At the house, we also found the missing piece of Mr Muir's gun together with a ring from the leg of a racing pigeon. And there were indeed traces of candle wax.

'My own view is that the fore-end and the ring may have been moved, but only so that they could be photographed from the window. Mr Russell takes a different view. As I have said, he is a very angry man. In his mind, he has convinced himself that those things were planted in order to support a trumped-up story for the defence. He refuses to see that Mrs Muir's confession invalidates at least a part of that supposition. He insisted on a fresh search for fingerprints, which is not yet finished, and he himself lifted the fingerprint which had been found and photographed inside the controls of the Muirs' alarms. When last I saw him, he was on his way to the room which he has been using in our building here, to fetch the photographs of that print and of the fingerprints which my sergeant obtained from you. In this,' Munro said with satisfaction, 'he will not succeed. Both have, unfortunately, been mislaid. He will undoubtedly come here next.'

Keith had had several weeks to worry about what story to tell if the worst should come to the worst. His best effort might be worth testing. 'When I was thinking of getting my own installation,' he said, 'Jake showed me the insides of a control box in the shop and told me how to reset the code. I tried it out for myself. I expect that's the box which ended up in the Muir house. That could explain my fingerprint, if it should happen to turn up.'

'That might stand up in court,' Munro said judicially, 'but I can think of many arguments against it. Could you explain how that print survived when the code was reset, several times, by others?'

'I'll have a bloody good shot at it,' Keith said. He humped his chair back to change his view through the window. 'Did you come in a jam sandwich?'

'I brought Mr Enterkin in my Jaguar.'

'Then Russell's here now.'

A ring on the doorbell lasted long beyond polite bounds. They heard Molly's footsteps tapping towards the front door.

'Shall I give him an earful?' Keith asked.

'You hold your wheesht,' Mr Enterkin said. 'When the

time comes, *I* shall give him an earful. That is what lawyers are for.'

Munro stirred in his chair. 'Do you wish me to go or to stay?'

'That,' Mr Enterkin said, 'would depend on your attitude. Do whichever you think I would want you to do.'

Chief Inspector Munro settled back in his chair.

Keith, Munro and Mr Enterkin were grouped at one end of the dining table. None of them rose when Chief Inspector Russell stamped in and thumped down, uninvited, into a chair at the far end of the table. In his anger, he had pulled himself up into a better posture than his usual almost hunchbacked stoop, and again Keith could see him as he must have been in his uniformed days, a formidable figure. His solid bulk and the vitality of his fury made his end of the table the head of it.

The glare which the big man directed at Keith could, Keith thought, have defrosted the late Mr Muir in a few seconds. 'I suppose you think you're damn clever,' he said.

Keith opened his mouth to say that, yes, he did think so. Mr Enterkin was quick to forestall him. 'Irrelevant,' the solicitor snapped. 'You've already wasted far more than enough of my time and that of my clients Messers Calder and Paterson, without entering into discussions of their opinions of themselves.'

Russell ignored him and looked at Munro. 'What are you doing here?'

'Visiting.'

'Stay. I may want a witness.'

'You should have brought Ritchie.'

Russell gave a snort of contempt. 'That man's an incompetent. Well up to scratch for the cowboy outfit you run out here, but he wouldn't last ten seconds in a city force. He's lost the records of those fingerprints, the ones which

189

could prove the house had been entered. As the officer in charge, I've been told to do a further investigation; and that's exactly what I'm going to do. And if I can prove unauthorized entry to that house, I'll have the advocate's office go before Lord Bickenholme and show that that evidence was planted.'

'Could have been planted,' said Mr Enterkin.

'Was,' said Russell. 'Was. Why else would Calder's fingerprint be inside the box?'

'It isn't.'

'It was. It's safe now between a piece of Sellotape and a card signed by four officers and on its way to Edinburgh. I came here to get a fresh set of Calder's prints.'

'You can't have them,' Mr Enterkin said.

'I can and I will.' Russell placed a wrapped object on the table. 'This is your glass back. I don't believe, Mr Calder, that the prints on it were yours. I believe that, accidentally or a-purpose, Ritchie made a guddle and took a wrong glass. I demand that you furnish me with a fresh set.'

Mr Enterkin managed a laugh, although Keith could see a very slight tremor in his hands. 'If the police have been careless enough to lose the first set, I do not see any obligation on my client to submit to being pestered for more prints until the cows come home. Your request is refused.'

'Then I shall take Mr Calder into custody on suspicion of attempting to pervert the course of justice.'

'That would be unwise,' Mr Enterkin said. 'It would force me to brief counsel to argue, first, that anything done in support of a case which Mrs Muir's confession now proves to be true must have been supporting rather than perverting the course of justice; and, secondly, that, almost in Lord Bickenholme's own words, what is sauce for the goose is sauce for the gander. Or, in this case, perhaps I should say sauce for the pigeon. I deny, of course, that my client introduced any evidence into the house, but counsel will argue that he might well have been justified had he done so, in view of your own fabrication of evidence concerning the microswitch.'

Russell did not even blink. 'I'd like to see you proving such a thing,' he said.

'You will see it, but you won't like it. We will start with an independent forensic examination of that switch, which turned up so unexpectedly and is now seen to run counter to all the true evidence. Was it, in fact, damaged in an explosion, or will our expert decide that you gave it a smack with a hammer? Will chemical analysis of the scorching upon it verify the presence of gunpowder, Nobel 80 and petrol? Or did you merely give it a few minutes in the fireplace?

'Next, was that component found in the first search, or did it turn up later, after your own expert had suggested the necessity of such a switch because the current generated in a radio-telephone would be inadequate to fire the explosion on its own? Will we discover that you were the happy searcher? Or will the officer who made the find withstand rigorous examination under threat of prosecution for perjury?'

Mr Enterkin paused. The others waited. Keith was aware of a new Ralph Enterkin. The mild, sometimes ineffectual solicitor, without raising his voice, had taken command. To interrupt would have been unthinkable.

'Finally,' he resumed, 'we would call on Miss Gurney, the assistant in Mr Paterson's shop. You were, of course, too careful to buy the component. But she saw you abstract such a switch from one of the display stands and is prepared to swear to it.'

Russell found his voice. 'She didn't,' he said. 'You were the one who mentioned perjury. It would be perjury for her to swear such a thing. She never saw it. It never happened.'

'She would be safe from a charge of perjury, because you could only prove that it was perjury by proving where you really obtained that component. Are you prepared to try that? Really, I am surprised at you for falling into such an elementary trap.'

'I don't know what you're talking about. What trap?'

'You said that Miss Gurney could not swear to having seen you steal the component because you had stolen it from quite a different shop.'

Russell was on his feet, and his voice made some silverware rattle on the mantelpiece. 'I never said any such thing.'

'I heard you,' Keith said. 'Distinctly.'

'Munro?'

Munro's grin was savage, showing his long teeth. He cupped his hand behind his ear. 'Pardon?' he said.

'Sauce for the pigeon,' Mr Enterkin repeated.

When Russell had stormed out, spitting threats which they all knew were empty, Keith said, 'I'll never slander that feather-brained bladder of lard again.'

'May I borrow your phone?' Mr Enterkin asked. 'I had better phone the good lady. She has no great love for you, but she is intensely loyal to her employer, and no doubt her loyalty will extend to the man who proved her boss innocent.'

Keith was only half listening. Now that another crisis seemed to be averted, his mind was already moving on. He was wondering what action to take against Bob Jack at Haizert, action which would incorporate a suitable measure of revenge. Keith hated to owe a grudge.